THINKING OUT LOUD

Keeping Nothing Behind

Tapan Ghosh

First published in 2021 by
BecomeShakespeare.com

One Point Six Technologies Pvt Ltd.
119-123, 1st Floor, Building J2, B - Wing, WadalaTruck Terminal, Wadala
East, Mumbai, Maharashtra, India, 400022.
T:+91 8080226699

ISBN: 978-93-5458-631-6

Cover designed: Tushar More

AUTHOR'S NOTE

The musings, recollections and stories in this collection represent moments that go back to the time when I was twelve years old. I cherish them because they transport me from a worldly existence to a subliminal one.

I hope you enjoy reading them and find yourself transported likewise.

PREFACE

Life is nothing but a bag full of simple joys, some instances of surprise, few crazy coincidences, and some melancholic days often disguised as destiny or suffering. *Thinking Out Loud - Keeping Nothing Behind* is a beauteous conglomeration of these multiple aspects of life, put together with a hint of philosophical perception by renowned author Tapan Ghosh.

It is the affiliation that the readers will find in author's understanding of varied facets of life in this book, which makes it an ideal choice to learn the art of positive response even in challenging situations.

With many of his published books in fiction and non-fiction genre, *Thinking Out Loud - Keeping Nothing Behind* stands apart with its completely unique approach towards life and beauty with which the author connects with his readers.

CONTENTS

YOU ARE A NOBODY

The real me knew nothing; it was only a kid. I stayed far away from that kid. He was more of a monkey.

I was right at the top of the ladder, everyone respected me. I had done well in life, I was definitely a *Somebody*, a force to reckon with, while he, a mere kid, was a *Nobody*.

What could I do with the Nobody in me? He made me sad. It was demeaning to be with him. I didn't want to ever think about him and that's why I tried to remain busy. I had so much to do. I travelled, met and talked to many important people. Thank God I was never alone, otherwise that fool would keep bothering me. No wonder they say that an empty mind is the devil's workshop.

Oh God! He *was* the devil. At night when I rested my head on a pillow, he bothered me by pervading my thoughts. I just could not get rid of him. I had sleepless nights. He was responsible for the dark circles under my eyes.

Then came a time when the world economy slowed down and the capital goods industry was hit tremendously. We all had to work 24/7 for mere survival. That took a heavy toll on me.

My age-old cervical spondylosis resurfaced. The nerve on the left side of the neck was completely blocked and I had to get it pressed hard by a novice therapist. When it opened suddenly, the rush of blood caused a sharp pressure-drop, resulting in a stoppage of oxygen supply to my brain. I was completely breathless.

I panicked because this would result in paralysis or death. At that moment, I wondered what would happen to my family and to others dependent on me.

This anxiety made me surrender to the inner me, the Nobody.

Nobody took over. He said that I was responsible for others being dependent on me. After my demise, they would be better off independent. This gave me a sense of relief. I smiled; the pressure had vanished. Nobody commanded me to take action, asking me to count my last breath. I did so myself, taking my time. I took another breath and then one more. The pace of my breathing slowly increased. I realised that because I was no longer anxious, my breathing resumed the normal rhythm soon enough.

I was put on oxygen and taken to an ambulance on a stretcher. Soon, my condition was normal, as if *nothing had happened*.

Today I am fitter than ever before. All this because I learnt a lesson by understanding my soul, the *Nobody* and its powers. On consulting an astrologer, I was told that my horoscope for that fateful day and time predicted a *Maran Tulya Kastha* (death-like experience).

As a result of this experience, that *Somebody* in me stands defeated. It has surrendered to the *Nobody* who had always been at daggers drawn with me. Apart from looking fitter and younger, I have adopted a positive approach to life. I now understand the meaning of surrendering our problems to God, the God within.

The real me is not a person, a Nobody

I am the important one, I am Somebody

Peer pressure will give me a false identity

The tussle within me will pull us down with gravity

While Somebody is full of complexity

Nobody makes you believe in simplicity

When Somebody creates problems that magnify

Nobody takes up those problems to simplify

If both of these must co-exist

One of them ought to virtually exit

While Nobody is faceless, without limit or restraint

For Somebody to be so, must be a criminal or a saint

Logic and passion in me are together

Like joining my hands in surrender

When my Somebody and Nobody merge

My energies amplify, I grow, I surge

The outer world is ruled by Somebody

But the inner world is ruled by Nobody

Discipline is the credo of the outer world

Whereas purity is the strength of the inner world

Your conscious, the Somebody, lives in the outer world

Whereas Nobody, your subconscious resides in the inner world

Somebody has all the concern

But Nobody will never yearn

Attachment is due to insecurity and is mind driven

Whereas pure love is causeless and is heart given

The mind is Somebody and the soul Nobody

The two will add up to make me Everybody

Nobody is your soul, heart, free-mind, inner-self or whatever you may call it. It resides on the right side of the brain, which is home to emotions, intuition, creativity, art, music, purity, faith, passion, illogical logic and the abstract. It is beyond worldly influence.

Somebody is your mind, the controlled mind or your outer self. It resides in the left side of the brain which accounts for logic, language, reasoning, analysis, maths and discipline and caters to worldly requirements.

The storage of memory and the control centre of all bodily functions is in the central part of the brain.

Power, that we hanker for, is not about controlling, but about being controlled by yourself.

The mind blocks the unconventional to remain in control, not realising that being free-spirited yields significant benefits.

A master is one who can effortlessly alternate between a free mind and a controlled one.

MYTHOLOGY AND RELIGION

Mythology, as it is called, is the knowledge from the scriptures of unknown antiquity. A study of the wisdom contained therein requires the seeker to undertake an inward journey. The knowledge thus acquired is so profound that it must be shared. It is almost a command from the beyond. How must it be shared, is the key question. People generally prefer knowledge in the form of tales that make the essence interesting and memorable. Over time, such stories become the gospel of truth and the basis of religion defined by a set of rules and a code of conduct.

Rigidity sets in and two classes of adherents emerge; enforcers and followers. The larger group comprises of followers who are made to believe that the privileged group of enforcers are the representatives of God with moral authority over them.

These power brokers enforce their authority through force and blind trust. History is replete with instances of wars fought in the name of religion. A religion becomes a set of rules made by the authorities for the believers to follow blindly. In doing so, most succumb to rituals as a means of influencing God for blessings. The very purpose of the profound knowledge is lost.

The issue is not about God being with us, as He is with everyone without discrimination. The question is, are *we* with God? Has God created us or is it the other way around?

Most of the sins are committed in the name of God. We are made to fear God. The moment you fear God; He is not God. God is but the creation of godmen. True God is within all of us, but we are too occupied with the outer world to look within.

A true man of God is one who keeps himself physically, mentally, emotionally and spiritually healthy. Only when you connect with yourself, you get the liberty to interact with the subliminal. Absorbing the scriptures within you is more virtuous than reading a prayer book. You will then see God within yourself and in others too.

We don't see God in others because it is easier to see the devil in them. Love changes all that and it starts by loving yourself. Only then you will accept the divinity in the people around you and grasp the true essence of the scriptures.

WHAT A COINCIDENCE!

'Coincidence is beyond logical explanation and hence understood only by the illogical part of the mind called heart.'

There are many incidents in my life that have made me believe so.

In fact, such incidents that we attribute to coincidences happen every now and then. If you look back and analyse, you will realise that there is a profound purpose to every such happening.

I will narrate one that took place about two decades ago. My wife had received an SMS message that had given her nightmares. It talked about performing certain rituals for *Santoshi Mata*. Further, the message said that the recipient should consider themselves blessed for having received the message. It urged the recipient to forward the same to 30 others who would do likewise in turn.

This gave my wife a sleepless night. First of all, she was not a believer in Santoshi Mata. Neither did she know which of her contacts were. She did not have too many contacts either and wanted to forward the message to some of my contacts too.

I told her that I was not willing to share my contacts with her. I tried my best to explain that these tricks were just a money-making racket on the part of the service providers.

We visited a temple to put forth our predicament to the Goddess *Santoshi Mata*. Typically, Hindu temples have many idols of God. The one we visited had a giant *Bajrangbali* right in the front and next to it was the lingam of *Lord Shiva* on one side and an idol of *Shri Ganesha* on the other. There were smaller statues of *Durga Mata*, *Laxmi Mata*, *Santoshi Mata* and other deities.

At the end of the temple were the statues of *navagrahas* (nine celestial bodies), these being the Sun, Moon, Mars, Mercury, Jupiter, Venus, Saturn, and the ascending and descending lunar nodes.

We rightfully have many manifestations of God as each one emphasises a particular human characteristic. We need all this to strike an inner balance.

As we stood in front of the idol of Goddess *Santoshi Mata* to seek pardon, we saw a woman in a torn sari, apparently needy, in front of us. She was down on her knees with tears flowing from swollen eyes, repeatedly calling out *'Jai Santoshi Maa'*.

We looked at each other and realised that it was best to offer all the money we had brought as an offering to the Goddess, to her follower. The woman's eyes sparkled on seeing our gesture, but she was reluctant to accept the large sum of money we offered. Then we told her that we had been *instructed* to hand it over to her.

She went back, thanking the Goddess for this miracle. Her faith was reinforced. This set our minds at rest and we came away feeling happy.

Everything happens for a good purpose. The purpose the mind comprehends is called ethics. What comes before it is morals; it is what your heart desires.

RAPISTS AT LARGE

We live in troubled times.

While there have been tremendous advances in many other spheres, our approach towards women remains in the Dark Ages. Our mind-sets haven't changed despite the free flow of modern technology and influences from across the globe. We still consider women as objects of sex. The gender inequality and male insecurity is turning us into a nation of potential rapists. This may be the right time to change the mind-sets by legalising prostitution.

Harry puts forth his arguments to change mind-sets.

Khush and Harry were buddies despite Harry being older by 15 years. After a tough game of tennis, they were cooling their heels at CCI. Harry ordered another round of coffee. This was his fourth cup since morning.

Khush: *Hey Harry, have you got addicted to coffee lately?*

Harry: *Have I? For that matter, Khush, you have been addicted to a woman lately. You have been with Natasha for over a month now.*

Khush (smiling): *I just want her to settle down after which she will be on her own. It's a matter of another fortnight.*

Harry: *Cool! Likewise, I want just a day more with coffee, till I get over my sore throat. No harm in getting addicted to someone or something, but only till such time as we want to and don't need to.*

Stagnant mind-sets lead to a deteriorating situation

Khush: *That's neat! Now tell me, with all the media uproar, will women ever be able to move about freely and safely in this country?*

Harry: *I doubt it, the rape scene may worsen further.*

Khush: *Why do you say so?*

Harry: *We need to question the mind-set of the people who frame and practise law. The law says a man is entitled to rape his wife. This is ridiculous, how can we outrage their modesty? It makes us amongst the most backward nations in the world.*

Khush: *I believe so, but why do you connect this to the rapist at large?*

Harry: *Why don't women have the same status and freedom that we men have? Why are they considered the weaker sex? Who are we to judge them and restrict them? Why do we hide our women and overly protect them?*

Woman - weaker sex, overly protected.

Men feel threatened by women

Khush: *Too many questions, Harry. Basically, you are saying that the answer to my question is quite deep-rooted.*

Harry: *That's right. Because we are threatened by them, we label them as the weaker sex. Most men are potential rapists, as they are mentally and emotionally weaker.*

Khush: *Absolutely Harry! What about the men who go in groups to attack a young girl? They are the weakest of the lot, the gang rapists.*

Harry (in disgust): *The bloody male domination comes out of such inferiority complex. Do you know about Hawa Mahal?*

Khush: *Not much, I only know it's a palace in Jaipur.*

Harry: *Women of the royal family who were under strict observance of purdah were allowed to witness royal processions and proceedings of the marketplace unseen by the outside world, through pigeonhole-like openings called jharokhas.*

Khush: *This is worse than slavery, Harry!*

The damage caused by denying human desires

Harry: *We have thus made them the objects of forbidden thoughts and unconscious desires. It is human nature to want what we cannot have or should not have. The more they are denied, the stronger is their desire. By making the laws more rigid, you might instigate a potential rapist.*

Khush: *Hmm, I see what you mean. But what do you think about women who solicit?*

Harry: *Forcing women into sex is like making money out of their rape, a gang rape. This is only because prostitution is not legalised, and women are not allowed to solicit. As long as it is mutual between two adults for money or basic needs, it's their business.*

Lots of cities have had illegal brothels from time immemorial.

A society of hypocrites

Khush: *You nailed it, Harry. Every city, big or small, has had illegal brothels, where underage – sometime even before they attain puberty – women kept in bondage, are constantly raped for money. Why is this a norm?*

Harry: *However, this is considered immoral by a society of hypocrites who are supported by laws made by people with double standards. Because of such rules and regulations, a vast section of men across India are frustrated and desperate to prove their manhood. As a result, there are countless incidents of rape every day and only a fraction of them get reported. The most degrading of them are the ones involving doctors and patients, priests and disciples, teachers and students, lawmakers and law enforcers, politicians and the public, householders and maids and sexual harassment at the workplace.*

A nation of potential rapists

Khush: *This makes a lot of sense. The men here are so frustrated and desperate for sex that they all are potential rapists. Sex is such a taboo that it is confined to illegal, unhygienic brothels. Like in the state of Gujarat, a dry state, alcohol is sourced from bootleggers.*

Harry: *Yes, Khush, that's a good analogy. It is simply a demand-and-supply issue. Legalising the trade would serve an entire community. Doctors in attendance will ensure the highest standards of hygiene and attract tourism. Taxation will boost the economy. It will eradicate illegal businesses run by corrupt politicians and the underworld.*

Khush: *This is a perfect plan to do away with disease, terrorism and funding for politicians and the underworld.*

Legalising prostitution – the only way out

Harry: *I am glad that these gruesome incidents have at least united people across the country. Gone are the days when love and sex were inextricably combined. The art of seduction was the poetry of life. But now, sex is only a bad word, thanks to our dirty minds. The basic need won't vanish, it will accumulate and inflate like a balloon till it bursts, and that's rape. In most cases, of course, it's their prostate that balloons up and if unattended, leads to prostate cancer.*

Khush: *Ha ha, that's a good one! You are so right, Harry. Unless we change our mind-set, there is no hope.*

Harry: *Yes. To change something so deep-rooted, we need to do something quite drastic. Remove restrictions and narrow-minded policies. Legalise prostitution.*

IS LOVE AN ILLUSION?

The world tells us that love is one of many emotions, a state of mind that is temporary and there is more to life than that. It made me wonder if it's really so. I began my search for an answer by running a search on the internet.

Looking for the answers

The search threw up some interesting answers. One of them said that being in love is a chemical state and an emotional one too. As the chemicals and emotions change, the state of being in love may change. This argument suggested that it could be of a temporary nature but made no reference to it being an illusion. Another said that, more than chemicals and emotions, it is defined by behaviour, which is real and backed by habit and reason. This source challenges the theory of love being an illusion.

My take on love

Well, it is no illusion simply because it feels real to the person in love. Transient or permanent, you feel and experience every effect of love. The high of a stolen glance, the low of a furious fight, the joy of spending time together and the sorrow of a betrayal are all the effects that we experience for real. This is not an illusion.

Love is not blind either

It does not blind you to the faults of your lover; it simply makes those faults more acceptable, thus creating a perfect environment for mutual respect and growth. The day that love fades away, these very eccentricities appear starker than they are and may be a bit too much for us to handle.

It is the perfect anaesthetic for our perceptions

We tend to be judgmental many times. It works as the perfect anaesthetic, numbing judgement to allow us to experience bliss in its purest form. It allows us to accept and be accepted without pressure or uninvited perceptions. It gives us the passion and strength to fight for our beloved and protect them from insult and harm.

Love overcomes social norms

With love, we care more about the needs and concerns of our loved ones, overriding social norms. Remember Romeo-Juliet, Shirin-Farhad and Heer-Ranjha? They didn't care about social standing, family ties, morality or riches – they simply cared for each other. The love of these couples was real, not an illusion.

How can something that produces such profound effects be an illusion?

It is probably the comforting factor that warms you when you come home from a hard day's work. The warm gulp of whisky that sets fire to your blood when you need a pick-me-up, the comfort food when you are feeling low and the soft breeze that caresses your cheek on a hot summer day, to name few.

How can something with profound effect be an illusion?

How can our existence, be a delusion?

The comfort that warms you, after a hard day's work,

The reassurance without which, life would go berserk.

With whom would you share, the happiest moments of your life?

The ups and downs, the struggles, the challenges and strife!

Who would you run to, in times of stress?

Who would reassure you, when the hardships oppress?

The comforting warmth, of the breath on your neck,

Without which you could turn, into a wreck,

Love is the reason we are alive, smiling and feeling,

Love is the balm that causes all healing,

Love is God, God is love, all-encompassing, without exclusion,

How can something so profound, be an illusion?

THE TRIPLE TALAQ BILL: A TIME FOR CHANGE

Khush: *Today's newspaper says that the Triple Talaq Bill will be a game-changer for Women's Empowerment in India. Sadly, it has run into opposition in the Rajya Sabha.*

Harry: *Why? What's the problem? Let's first understand the full implications of the Bill. It is necessary to know what it proposes.*

Khush: *The Bill makes the pronouncement of talaq-e-biddat null and void. The pronouncement could be by words, either spoken or written or in electronic form or in any other manner whatsoever. Any man doing so is liable to be punished with a jail term of up to three years and a fine. Further, it makes the pronouncement of talaq-e-biddat a non-bailable offence.*

Harry: *Furthermore, the Bill aims to put an end to the instant and irrevocable nature of marital ties which form a bedrock of human relationships. The Bill proposes that the woman upon whom talaq is pronounced, will receive an allowance from her husband, and retain custody of her children.*

Khush: *Opposition parties have objected to the clause that provides for a jail term, arguing that it could further strain ties between the principal parties and diminish the ability of the husband to provide sustenance while serving a jail term. Opposition from the community leaders is based on the premise that the Bill impinges on practices sanctioned by religion and which have been followed for centuries. As a counterpoint, it may be said that 22 Islamic countries have already banned the practice of triple talaq.*

Harry: *The Bill is a landmark development in empowering women. The institution of marriage must be based on the principal of equality between the two partners. Any practice that puts one in a position of advantage over the other is clearly hostile to the times. More so, in a democratic country like India, where the constitution treats every citizen as an equal, the Triple talaq impinges on women's individual rights and shuts out room for discussion and resolution.*

Khush: *It's time to be in step with the times.*

SADLY, LOVE AND MARRIAGE GO TOGETHER LIKE HORSE AND CARRIAGE

The horse signifies love. The love tied to a carriage, which is the burden of marriage. Lovers get bound for a purpose and it's no longer love because love is purposeless. Marriage conforms to social norms. A sense of duty and responsibility comes into play. On the other hand, love between soulmates is profound. It can defy such norms because it has no set boundaries or restraints. If you are in love and marriage is your goal, it's not love. Marriage is a contract. Love is a journey, not a destination like marriage.

True love is generally between those whose circumstances are contrasting. For this reason, society looks down upon such unions. Peer pressure does not allow love to survive. Laila-Majnu and Romeo-Juliet are cases in point. Unless you take your love to another level, to that of *Radha* and *Krishna* - the profound love transcends all definitions. It is so profound that it cannot be bound by any sense of duty. It flows spontaneously, overcoming all barriers.

Soulmates come into your life for a good reason, to put you on the right path. The journey can be enjoyable if you have faith. Love acts as a catalyst for a growth in individual character. Love has no room for attachment as it is free and cannot be possessed. This is the toughest lesson to learn in life.

Freedom from attachment begins by understanding that self-attachment is nothing but ego and only an egoless person will love his own self. One become egoless only when self-attachment turns to love.

This is easier said than done. You have to indulge yourself. You may even experience heartbreaks to understand your own self. Only then will you will be sympathetic towards yourself, instead of longing for sympathy. This will teach you to love yourself. The mind will move towards the heart, the inner self, the God within. Then you don't need anything because you achieve everything. You are in love. You find love everywhere. You don't limit your love to a person. Love is God and God is everywhere.

For instance, if a man relishes the apple his soulmate eats, he is in love. He cherishes everyone and everything his soulmate loves. This is true love, which is unconditional. *'The Radha-Krishna love story is an instance of the zealous pursuit of spirituality springing forth eternally from the individual self towards the universal self.'* (Speaking Tree: Why Krishna never married Radha?)

There are lessons to be learnt from this. The way to conquer life is by living on the edge of a precipice called love. To conquer love is to eradicate attachment. Life is bliss with detached attachment.

THE TRUTH ABOUT ASTROLOGY

There is much confusion about astrological predictions. An astrologer's reputation vacillates a lot. Sometimes, he is the messenger of God and at other times a fraudster, depending on his predictions going right or wrong. Not only the person but the profession itself is denounced. When a doctor, engineer or any other professional goes wrong, do we lose our faith in the profession they represent?

Likewise, astrology is based on astronomy.

Astronomy is the study of the universe beyond the Earth's atmosphere. Astronomers examine the positions, motions and properties of celestial objects. Astrology attempts to study how those positions, motions and properties affect people and events on Earth.

Therefore, go by astrological (the logic in astrology) predictions by using your own reasoning. Ascertain the astronomical facts and the astrologer's take on the effect these have on you. Don't get influenced by him, you know yourself better than he does.

Don't expect the astrologer to predict the end result, as it depends on you to a large extent. His predictions are based on astronomical facts and the effect they have at large. Your results depend on what you do.

"Life is a sail boat ride and wind, the destiny. But dammit, you are the sailor!" - Tapan Ghosh

An astrologer can give you the magnitude and the direction of the wind, but it is for you as a sailor to decide how to propel the sailboat to your destination. The astrologer tells you about destiny. You have to leverage that knowledge to get to your destination.

Before setting off on the Everest expedition, Tenzing and Hillary consulted a priest who told them that neither of them would surmount Everest and he further predicted that one of them would die during the gruelling expedition. The duo defied the seer's prediction and went on to become the first men to stand atop the world's highest mountain on May 29, 1953.

This is where we need to understand the role of an astrologer. He can tell us about destiny, the course of events that will happen but he is in no position to predict the result. He can only say what might happen. Ultimately, you are the judge as no one knows you better than yourself. Forewarned is forearmed. We can defy the astrologer. This is what Tenzing and Hillary did. They prepared themselves for the climb to ensure that there would be no surprises for them. Think of a similar instance in your life and you will realise that it was your initiative that propelled you to your destination.

Climbing the mountain was the less difficult part for Tenzing and Hillary. Making it back to the base camp alive was the bigger challenge. The same is true of life, as stated in the quote below.

"Reaching great heights is not half as tough as coming down in life with your sanity intact." - Tapan Ghosh

DOUBLE STANDARDS DOUBLE OMELETTE

What's your take? We live with double standards, applying a different set of norms to men and women. This creates artificial differences and makes women vulnerable to the worst forms of exploitation. Over a double omelette breakfast, Harry and Khush call for a change in mind set.

Harry and Khush had just finished their breakfast of double omelettes made to their individual liking. Khush preferred them with cheese and tomatoes while Harry avoided diluting the taste of eggs with add-ons. His was a plain omelette instead, rolled and well done.

Khush: *Nice and fulfilling.*

Harry: *Nice, yes! But fulfilling, with just two eggs? I am sure you can do better.*

Khush: *Maybe Harry. You seem to know a lot about me.*

Harry: *Sure, I do (seeing another omelette being brought from the kitchen). Don't worry, this is your kind of omelette, not my type. Ramu knows I don't go for a second helping.*

Khush: *Why don't you join in?*

Harry: *More than two eggs for me, are you crazy? I am not as young as you.*

Khush: *Whoever said that? You look younger than me.*

Harry (smiling): *Well, I still can't eat more because I need to fit into my slim-fit shirts.*

Khush was almost half way through his omelette when he grabbed the chicken sausages that had just arrived. Being health-conscious, Harry kept away from them too.

Remembering an old friend

Harry: *I just remembered a Parsi friend from college, Adi Shroff. Have I told you about him before?*

Khush: *I think you are trying to take a dig at me. I knew Adi Manik, not this guy. Okay, tell me about him.*

Harry: *Why did you think I was making fun of you? I wasn't, but something did remind me of a funny incident. We always laughed at Adi's expense but he didn't care, he was just amused. This is an impressive trait among Parsis; they even enjoy making fun of themselves.*

Khush was enjoying his last bite of omelette with bread and butter. Harry would spread olive oil, not butter, on his whole wheat bread, or sometimes have his omelette with chapattis.

Main course after dessert

Harry: *Adi was a great guy like you, but sadly, he is no more. He died twenty years ago in California. Once, Adi, I and a few friends, all engineering students, went to a fancy restaurant for dinner. We had an elaborate six-course meal and topped it up with dessert. After a while, Adi asked for mutton biryani and the waiter got it in a jiffy.*

What's this? Adi enquired.

Mutton biryani, replied the waiter.

What?! Adi was shocked to see a carry bag on the table.

Parcel kiya, saab.

Who told you to parcel it? Roared Adi at the waiter.

Saab, aap sab ne khana kha liya. Kitna pet bharke khaya, main dekh raha tha. Baad main aap ne itna cake bhi khaya aur ice cream bhi. Iske baad kaun biryani kha sakta hai? Isliye maine pack kiya.

Kyun pack kiya? Kaun bola? Main kitna bhi khaoon, tumhare baap ka kya hai? Don't waste my time, jaldi serve karo.

Harry: *All of us had a hearty laugh. The poor waiter who looked offended actually had a smile on his face. Adi became famous overnight in the university hostel.*

Khush (laughing loudly): *Oh! I remind you of Adi.*

Harry: *In more than one way he was smart-looking, jovial and a good soul like you.*

Maid service or the unmaking of man?

Khush (drawing Harry's attention to the well-endowed maid who was serving them): *I think we need to be careful here.*

Harry (smiling): *I wonder if this is how Shiney Ahuja got enticed.*

Khush (reading Harry's mind): *Well, Shiney is not the only one; there are others, who don't get exposed because they managed to hush up things. They say Shiney just walked into a trap.*

Harry: *Yes, this is a racket with the support of cops. They plant a sexy maid to lure a man who is alone in the house and then create a scene. The cop land up and extort. If you don't pay up, you end up like Shiney.*

Guilty or Innocent

Khush: *When I say this, I don't mean Shiney is innocent. I don't know about him. I only know what the media tells us. But I do know about some others who were subjected to extortion.*

Harry: *The laws have become tougher to protect women and the cops are going to take full use of them. The innocent ones are going to pay the price. You are absolutely right; all the maid has to do is dial a cop and her word will be final. All she has to say that we stripped her naked with our eyes. The new law is going to protect them against everything.*

Khush: *This is crazy, but hopefully, women are going to be safe after all.*

Harry: *Bullshit. Nothing is going to stop the hard-core rapist who will resort to hit-and-run tactics.*

Legalising prostitution – the only way forward?

Khush: *What is the solution? Last time we spoke about this, you said legalising prostitution is the only way out.*

Harry: *Not just that, people must change their mindsets. It is an age-old universal issue, predominant in conservative countries like ours. This is surfacing now because the rapidly-growing middle class is making a hue and cry about it and the media is supporting them. Down the centuries, women have suffered injustice. They have always been treated as showpieces and meant for producing children. In Victorian times, women going to the washroom would excuse themselves for powdering their nose. Men viewed them only as sexual objects, the thought of them wanting or enjoying sex was not known or even considered.*

This was the birth right of the male alone. It's only in the past fifty years or so, and that too, only in the most affluent societies that women have gradually overcome the guilt of enjoying intercourse imposed on them. Some lucky ones have even experienced climax. This has made men insecure. As is, they need ego boosting all the time. The woman has to fake a climax with all the oohs and aahs to satisfy the male ego.

Why place the burden on women?

Why do women have to bear children? Because, their husbands will not be considered men, otherwise. Why are women more ambitious than men, in general? Because they are brought up like that. They grow up being told they are the inferior sex, incapable of matching men. Because it's a man's world. A woman is respected when she bears a male child. The birth of a girl is considered a curse. Their families want to get rid of them before they are conceived. They are married off quickly before puberty. Men are considered men only when they hit upon women. Why isn't that freedom given to women too? Society is dominated by insecure men. Their EQ is generally lower than that of women.

The damaging impact of media

One of the repercussions of media – especially, TV and social media – is that more youngsters are being attracted to big cities; especially, women. They adopt the morals of the west to rationalise their behaviour. Young girls from middle-class families get mesmerised by the glamour of big cities and many of them end up in dance bars or the flesh trade. In order to justify their actions and fulfil their responsibilities, they send part of their earnings home.

The successful ones get their freedom and status by being the breadwinners of their families. Some of the bright ones even invest wisely or start a new venture and gain respectability sooner or later, abandoning their previous lives completely. The not-so-smart ones have a miserable time once they grow older. For that matter, any profession where looks matter has diminishing returns as you age. Therefore, if you aren't smart enough to have a parallel income or find a stable companion, you could be in trouble trying to maintain the standard of living you have gotten used to.

Most of the lower middle-class girls and boys are so naive and innocent, they need guidance. This is especially so of teenagers who are so influenced by the glamour of media that they run away from their homes in search of freedom and to get what they aspire for. Only the strong-minded ones are able to control themselves and become achievers.

Finding solutions

Khush: *What happens to the vast majority of them?*

Harry: *They should be our biggest concern. They are the victims of the vultures in our society.*

Khush: *What do we do with these sex-perverts?*

Harry: *We ought to find outlets for them. Legalising prostitution is a solution but only a small one.*

Khush: *What then?*

Harry: *We have to create jobs! Make in India and Skill India is a perfect idea.*

Khush: *But nothing is happening, most of them are losing jobs! Why? What happened to the promises made? Acche din ayenge, where's that?*

Harry: *Acche din aate nahin, laaye jaate hain. We all must have faith in the government. Big companies must invest in the Make in India platform.*

Khush: *Is that the solution for correcting sex perverts?*

Harry: *Sure. The emotion of sex is a state of mind. Because of ignorance on the subject and improper influences, this state of mind is generally associated with the physical. We need to transmute this energy.*

Khush: *Wow! Is this true?*

Harry: *Yes! The desire for sex is the most powerful of human desires. The transformation of these desperadoes to a very skilled and a productive lot is a definite possibility.*

FAITH AND RELIGION

We often think of faith and religion to be the one and the same thing. But is it really so? Does every religious person have faith? And is everyone who has faith in someone or something, religious? The author sets out to understand these concepts and provide the answers.

Harry: *Hey Khush, I've been asked to write an article on religion and faith.*

Khush: *Religion and faith; aren't the two the same? A strong belief in a supernatural power.*

Harry: *Hmm, yeah. What can I say that's not there already?*

Khush: *Well, you are the writer, Harry.*

Harry: *Quite so. Religion is man-made whereas faith is a spiritual concept.*

Khush: *I don't have faith in religion that is codified by the beliefs of religious bodies involved in politics and power struggles.*

Harry: *You are not alone in this. Religion gives rise to wars and conflicts around the world.*

Khush: *Hmm yeah, terrorism too.*

Harry: *So, what's your take on faith?*

Khush: *Faith is your own belief that may be based on logical thinking and experience.*

Harry: *True, but blind faith should be avoided as it can lead to specious reasoning.*

Khush: *So now, what are you going to say? What **is** your religion? Do you consider yourself religious?*

Harry: *I'm religious but there is no code of conduct or ritual that I follow.*

Khush: *Hmm, alright, so you have told me what you don't do. Now, tell me what you do.*

Harry: *I do everything religiously and sometimes get involved in the strangest of incidents. But I don't like to talk about them.*

Khush: *You are a writer, what will you write about, if you don't reveal yourself?*

Harry: *Hmm, okay buddy. Let me tell you what happened a few days ago. A vendor was trying to sell me a ten-rupee lottery ticket; I bought it just to please him.*

Khush: *Don't tell me! And…did you win?*

Harry: *No, silly. What will I do with the money? I have absolutely no use for it; I gave the ticket to the first urchin I saw.*

Khush: *Wow, so did he get lucky?*

Harry: *I don't know. Besides, the chances are one in a million, although I could see hope on his face. I felt bad, I told him that the chances were remote and gave him a thousand-rupee note. He was thrilled. I realised that I had done something crazy. As a reflex action I made him sit in the car and drove off.*

Khush: *Thank your stars, you saved yourself from a mob of urchins. This is just typical you! To do something like this.*

Harry: *Well, then I asked him what he was going to do with the money. He said he would return it to me the day he wins the lottery.*

Khush: *That was very thoughtful. You seem to attract good people. Otherwise, a guy like you cannot survive in this world.*

Harry: *Maybe! The guy told me how he planned to invest the thousand rupees. He wanted to earn money for his folks and now I had given him this big break. I dropped him back, hiding my tears behind my dark sunglasses. A lottery can do a great deal for the most deserving, for those who have been denied their due.*

Khush: *I see where you are coming from, Harry.*

Harry: *However, easy money can be a curse for most of us. It can only induce greed and make you its slave.*

Khush: *The insecure lot, the hoarders.*

Harry: *True, the wrong doers too, the power-hungry lot.*

Khush: *So, what's the moral of the story?*

Harry: *If you happen to win a lottery or have more than you need, put it to the most rewarding use. Be very selective; give it to the most deserving. You will feel blessed on seeing the joy on their faces. This is the biggest reward you can ever get. Do this with whoever your heart leads you to, without restriction or dos and don'ts. You should be a giver, enjoy distributing love. Love with an open heart, free of guilt. Follow the scripture in your heart, not the books alone.* **This**... *should be your religion. You may be called a fool by some and a cheat by others. It may be difficult for you to survive this way but if you do, I assure you, you will experience bliss.*

Khush: *Wow, that's good. Do you have something to say about faith?*

Harry: *Yes, a lot. But some other day.*

TO MAKE YOUR LIFE PURPOSEFUL, MAKE YOUR MIND PURPOSELESS

The only purpose of life is love. Love is pure. Love is God. Love is without purpose.

But the mind is purposeful. It absorbs information, transforms it into knowledge and acts accordingly. Most of the time it is so crammed with information that there is virtually no room for the infusion of fresh knowledge. We refuse to let go of our blocks, superstitions, grudges and beliefs that are no longer relevant.

The ever-changing nature of life gives us the opportunity to eliminate the obsolete and irrelevant in us through new experiences. Such experiences should refine or replace our existing knowledge for us to remain relevant at all times. Think of this as being similar to the periodic replacement of lubricant to keep the machine in running order.

In order to fulfil our existence in the worldly sense, we need to compromise. The heart represents purity, faith and passion while the mind stands for discipline, logic and analysis. The purposeful mind must combine with the purposeless heart to achieve the golden mean.

Through this golden mean, we can move closer to a mind without motive. This should be the purpose of our life.

OFFSIDE AT PARK-CIRCUS MAIDAAN, CALCUTTA

Football matches at the Park Circus Maidaan are a common sight. The ground has six pitches, most of them occupied during summer evenings by local teams made up of college-going players. Passers-by tend to linger a while, expressing support for one team or another. Those keen to follow a full game squat on the grass around the periphery of the pitch, inching into the playing area as the game progresses. They are so close to the action that they are almost a part of it. It's like watching a play where your seat is adjacent to and on the same level as the stage. However, unlike a theatre, you have to be alert at all times, lest a ball hit you.

That evening was no different. The Anglo-Indian Park Union team was playing in red jerseys and the *Desh Bandhoos* in blue. All attention seemed to be riveted on them. Other teams, playing without proper uniforms, came across as ragged outfits in comparison. Most of the spectators being Bengali-speaking, were *Desh Bandhoo* supporters. They cheered the team no end. An unusual sight that evening was the presence of a sizeable number of enthusiastic Anglo-Indian girls among the spectators.

Dada and the Anglo-Indian – the first contact

Dilip dada *(elder brother)*, as he was called, was captaining the *Desh Bandhoos*. Eighteen-year-old Dilip was a big brother indeed. A hooligan and a bully, everyone feared him. As the whistle blew, he took control of the ball. Playing centre-forward with nimble footwork, he dribbled well. Moving skilfully past his opponents, he was in possession of the ball for almost a minute before passing it to his left-in, who managed to take control after some hic-ups. The left-in was a fast runner; he took charge and move towards the dee. The opponents offered good defence as they seemed to be a better team. Dilip was desperately waiting for a pass but it was almost a lost cause by the time he got one. It took a huge effort from him to dive to a header to score that goal. The crowd erupted into cries of *'dada, dada.'*

What a beauty!

An Anglo-Indian lady gave Dilip a beaming smile. *'What a beauty!'* thought Dilip, as their eyes met before another youthful girl whispered something in her ear. He recalled the presumably young girl standing near their goal post with her friends, while the *Desh Bandhoo* players were changing for the match. Being a make-shift football pitch, there were no changing rooms on the ground. The players hadn't taken kindly to this intrusion and Dilip- whom the girls were scrutinising – had done something drastic. As if by accident, he had pulled down his football shorts to reveal something that had them scandalised. They had shot off immediately, much to the amusement of Dilip's team mates who had had a hearty laugh, *'dada, ki chomotkaar.'*

A sudden turn of events

However, the tables turned on *Desh Bandhoo* as the game progressed. Park Union were now able to exercise their defence and score without much effort. The Anglo-Indian girls were proving to be a great distraction in their miniskirts, playing cheer leaders every time Park Union scored a goal. With the leg show and the lusty cries of the spectators, Dilip and his mates could hardly concentrate on their game. It almost appeared to be a losing cause.

What happened next was not in the spirit of the game. A major dispute broke out as the referee wrongly called an offside. Supporters from either side invaded the pitch and beat up the referee before attacking the players. As a result, the game degenerated into a fight between the two sides and their supporters. Given the sheer number of supporters, *Desh Bandhoos* held the upper hand. The situation was indeed grave for the Anglo-Indian women; their safety was in question. Sensing the danger, Dilip headed in the direction of the Anglo-Indian lady who had smiled at him, placed her on his broad shoulders and ran to the safety of a building across the road. The wail of police sirens drowned out her screams.

Getting out of control

Dilip rushed to a balcony on the first floor of the building. He put the lady down, but held on to her hand in a firm grip. The lady landed a tight slap across his left cheek. This shook him up.

He was about to retaliate when the lady screamed, *'you want to rape me, you scoundrel. 'Why have you brought me here?'* she screamed again. Dilip did not know what to say, he just tried to calm her down but she wriggled out of his grip. Her looks mesmerised him and he started to move towards her.

'Stay away from me,' she screamed and he stopped dead. She is a strong woman, he thought. *'Listen, I am sorry. Please don't scream or create a scene.'* he said. Composing herself, she looked down at the scene below and exclaimed, *'oh my God!'*

An unexpected misunderstanding

By now the police had assumed control and were busy rounding up the rioters and the girls. Dilip saw her concern. He wanted to calm her down, but at the same time he was aching to take her in his arms.

'Don't you dare touch me,' she exploded like a lioness, *'I am old enough to be your mother.'*

He was aghast in disbelief. He noticed her looking at the girls. The police were handcuffing them before leading them to the police van. She looked at Dilip sternly and again looked at the scene below in helplessness. *'I am their teacher and look what I have done,'* she said and broke down. Dilip was shaken up. He was dying to make amends and struggling to think of a way to help her out of this mess.

'It's not wise for me to go down now, they will arrest me too. How will that help?' she said.

'I will do, whatever you…you…' Dilip started to stammer, his desire to be in her arms grew ten-fold. Dilip saw her look of disgust as she told him *'you have such a dirty mind, you deliberately undressed me in front of my students.'*

Operation Rescue

'I am sorry, I didn't mean to, it was just a reflex action in the heat of the moment. I will do whatever you say now,' said Dilip.

'Let's go to the police station to bail them out.' she commanded. Dilip sprang into action. He ran down and she after him. He hailed a

rickshaw and they quickly headed towards the police station.

Cindy's and Dada's minds were racing as the rickshaw sped to the police station. The vehicle had its destination cut out; the passengers were unsure of their own.

It was a classic clash of the perceptions of two opposing cultures. What seemed right to Dilip Dada was unacceptable to Cindy and vice versa. Each acted based on their own upbringing and thinking, not realising that their actions would be misconstrued as offensive by the other. What is one supposed to do in such situations? Stay calm and do nothing? That wasn't possible either. The situation was getting out of hand and some remedial action was necessary. According to you, how could the situation have been handled better?

ARE WE BALANCED?

Every object in the universe, despite moving through space at a hectic speed, is balanced. The world at large, is balanced. The bodies of all living creatures are balanced; the left side is balanced with the right. Engineering draws from nature and demands static balancing before dynamic balancing. Aerospace Engineering (Rocket Science) is nothing but static and dynamic balancing. The working principle is that of a firework rocket, which, as per Newton's Third Law of Motion, postulates that *to every action there is an equal and opposite reaction.*

The best example of nature's static balancing is a tree whose roots grow deeper and wider as it grows higher. The expanding roots make the foundation strong enough to balance the size and shape above the ground. We have yet to create this technology that allows the simultaneous construction of a structure and its foundation.

If everything is so harmonious about nature, why do natural calamities occur?

The problem lies with the human mind, which is unbalanced and the source of conflict. Our unbalanced mind is responsible for interference with nature. It is this action to which natural calamities are the reaction.

The left side of the brain is the rational side, which we call the controlled mind, while the right side is the emotional part, which may be referred to as the free mind. The controlled mind is based on reasoning and logic. It teaches us survival tactics, social norms and ethics. It understands science and mathematics. The free mind is illogical and it thrives on art and creativity.

Most of us are one-sided, hence unbalanced. This gives rise to conflict. The closer we get to the centre, the better off we will be. The ideal would be the golden mean between the two.

To achieve this balance, we must understand the positive and the negative aspects of the controlled mind and the free mind. While the controlled mind gives rise to negative traits such as attachment, ego, insecurity, fear, jealousy, greed and aggression, it also inculcates discipline, stability, reliability and ethical behaviour.

The free mind can be naive, childish, silly and unstable, with a propensity for monkeying around. On the other hand, it retains the purity of the new-born. It is the repository of faith, creativity, positivity and morals.

We are born with a free mind, but when the umbilical cord is cut, Newton's First Law of Motion applies to us. *Everybody continues in the state of rest or of uniform motion, unless acted upon by an external force to change its state.* Social norms act as the external force to make us worldlier. The controlled mind assumes charge.

With maturity comes wisdom.

This helps us control our mind and lead a life that is both adventurous and stable. As we approach the completion of our life's orbit, some of us enjoy the pleasures of reliving the purity of our childhood.

To bring harmony back into our lives, we must strike a balance within ourselves and create a sense of order. Our unstable mind is the cause of all the chaos in the world.

THE TRUTH ABOUT FAITH AND RELIGION

Continuing the discussion, this time Harry answers his son Arjun's queries about faith and religion. Do miracles occur in our lives? Or, are they confined to the scriptures alone? What is the cause of misery? What role do the fundamental laws of nature play in determining our lot? How does one achieve a state of bliss?

Harry provides answers to these questions and more about faith and religion, in a free-wheeling chat over a drink in a first-class lounge at Bombay International Airport.

First dream, then do!

Arjun: *Dad you were the first to convert the Bajaj Tempo to a luxury traveller, when I was little. My friends still talk about it.*

Harry: *Oh, that! Yes, that turned out good.*

Arjun: *Very sleek bedroom with a big LED TV, a bar, a lounge and a workplace with beds convertible to comfortable chairs and pull-out tables with computers.*

Harry: *Yes. And you know what, Chabria was going to make one for Jayalalita but I beat him to it. I made mine using some factory workers and a skilled carpenter. And that was a long time ago. There was no LED, the TV screen was LCD.*

Arjun: *Oh yeah, what did Chabria have to say?*

Harry: *He came to study the way I'd made my plans, with an extra dynamo on the same pulley to run my air conditioning system and refrigerator. He was sceptical about it and said they were not feasible with a Bajaj Tempo and that he'd believe me only when he saw it work. I told him that it was like building castles in the air. Only when you dream, can you work towards materializing it.*

Arjun: *I know, it's one of your favourite sayings and it always works for you.*

Harry: *It will work for you too, just stretch your imagination and believe in yourself. You are a smart lad Arjun, have faith in yourself.*

Faith, Religion and God – how are they connected?

Arjun: *Thanks, Dad. I will. Talking of faith, the other day Khush told me that you were discussing religion. That's strange! That's unlike you. I have never heard you talk about it.*

Harry: *What about faith?*

Arjun: *Faith, maybe, but not religion.*

Harry: *Hmm, well, every religion talks about faith.*

Arjun: *Do you believe in God?*

Harry: *God is subjective; how do you define God? Everyone's idea of God is very personal.*

Arjun: *A creator. God has created us.*

Harry: *We have created God! Our needs, our fears have created God.*

Arjun: *I don't believe in all this rubbish, please don't mention this in anyone's presence, they will think you are crazy. (After a pause) I am sorry, I vented out like this.*

Harry: *Don't worry, I won't. With you, it's different. We generally speak our heart out.*

Harry: *I don't know what I am, this is just my point of view and I am no one to say that I am right.*

Arjun: *Do you mind taking this further? I want to know how you think.*

Harry: *Sure, I know you have a mind of your own and no one can influence you.*

Are religious practices wrong?

Arjun: *Are you saying that we all are wrong in following religious practices?*

Harry: *No, not at all. It's your belief, a perfect way of life. It gives you solace, peace and the strength to face life. This faith gives you hope and positivity. Whatever works for you is great. As long as you don't pray for a purpose and expect God to solve all your problems because you've given dakshina to the priest. I don't believe in these miracles. These are mere figments of your imagination.*

Arjun: *I agree with you but these miracles do happen, there are all kinds of stories and some of us have witnessed them. You can't say that it's not possible.*

Harry: *Everything is possible, the mind being strong enough to make anything happen, even miracles, provided you have belief and complete faith. We even have quantum physics to tell you that the wave-particle duality is the doing of the mind. But why do we seek miracles? For reassurance that God is with us? Isn't the entire universe a miracle? The sun, the moon, the sky. Is that not enough to reassure you? We must pray to God with our actions, and that too causelessly. What's the point in time-consuming rituals and praying for miracles?*

Mother Nature – the root of all balance

Arjun: *So, you do believe in God?*

Harry: *Yes, I do. My God is Mother Nature. I need to get close to nature. Its laws govern us. From the time you are born, the laws of the universe govern everything from the physical to the mental, emotional and spiritual. From atoms and molecules to planetary systems, everything is so fluid and dynamic and yet stationary. Everything is in complete harmony. Santulan!*

Arjun: *Equilibrium! I remember when I was seven years old you took me on a flight to Sydney and how everyone laughed when I asked why the plane had stopped moving.*

Harry: *Yes, I remember they were serving lunch and the aircraft was cruising at forty thousand feet. It was so stable, it seemed to be stationary.*

Santulan – the balancing of forces

Arjun: *Yes, it felt as if it was not moving. You said it was; only the forces were balanced. I remembered this and much later, I studied thermodynamics. I knew how the lift, the vertical component of drag balanced the gravity, making the aircraft fly straight and level. The skill of the pilot was evident in flying with zero acceleration and the slightest gradient to produce just enough lift for the passengers to eat their lunch in comfort.*

Harry: *That is a perfect analogy, son; this is exactly how nature balances and keeps us all in equilibrium. The universe is so dynamic and yet so static. The two balance one another. Santulan! From the time we are born, we follow these laws subconsciously.*

A baby tries to walk, falls and learns how to cope with the laws of gravity. We learn everything from doing things. Life is a learning ground. The more you do, the more you fail. That's learning by trial and error. We learn to coexist with love, exactly like atoms and molecules. Complete bonding in love.

In the process, we must guard against running away from ourselves. Social pressures are the conflicts that we grow with. We cannot detach ourselves from our surroundings. We have to learn to balance, that's what nature is all about. Therefore, when you ask me about God, all I can think of is Mother Nature. We need to be as close to nature as possible. Newton's first and third laws of motion tells us a lot about it. We all know about third law and its significance. Tell me the first law.

The laws of the universe

Arjun: *Every object continues in the state of rest or of uniform motion unless acted upon by an external impressed force to change its state.*

Harry: *Yes, but what's the external force? Gravity in science, peer pressure in society. Without this, you are beyond worldly pressures. You are in space, beyond the escape velocity of earth.*

Arjun: *But who has created the universe? The laws of nature? Who has created nature? The Creator, God.*

Harry: *Why does anyone have to create nature; it is self-created. Okay, let us say that we will go with what you say. God created nature, the universe and multiple universes. He has given us everything. We only need to abide by the laws of the universe to be happy. You are answerable only to your soul, the God inside you. Your destiny is governed by the universe; it is tailor-made for you. The day that umbilical cord is cut, you are independent. It is for you to benefit. The Creator has done everything for your benefit and now everything is left to you. Do not bother Him now, just indulge in action and abide by the laws of the universe for complete bliss.*

Why so much misery all around?

Arjun: *In that case, why is there so much misery all around?*

Harry: *Because we seldom follow the laws of nature, the laws of the universe. The norms of society decide our actions. We do what is expected of us by our peers, passed off as God's will. We are always trying to prove ourselves worthy and, in the process, living a lie. The grip of attachment and ego leads to increased expectation and to greed, anxiety and fear, in turn. These insecurities make us miserable and we curse our luck, our destiny. At this stage we think of God and pray for solutions.*

Arjun: *Do you believe in heaven with God up there and the Devil down under in hell?*

Harry: *I accept your belief in God, but when you say up there, I don't know what you are talking about.*

Arjun: *How do you work towards going to heaven when you die?*

Harry: *You don't go anywhere, even when you die. Just look out of the window. If you don't believe you are in heaven now, to hell with you. Heaven and hell are one as both are right here, nowhere else. If you believe life is hell, it certainly is so.*

Arjun looks dumb founded, staring at his dad in disbelief. Harry smiles at him. His eyes are fixed on Arjun, studying his expressions. He nods in reassurance as his smile broadens.

What's your view? on Faith and Religion

So, both Heaven and Hell are within you. Bliss lies in being in harmony with Mother Nature, while going against the laws of the universe can invite misery. This is the immutable truth but each of us interprets it in their own way. What's your take?

HOLY COW!

At CCI, Harry and Khush were coming out of the tennis court holding their rackets. Seemingly exhausted, Harry said to Khush, *"What happened to you today! You were playing your shots so well that you gave me a good workout for a change."*

Khush laughed. *"You don't give up, do you? I decided to win the last set and I had to do everything I could to make that happen,"* he replied.

Harry made a face. *"Let's go for breakfast, I am starving,"* Khush continued. This was a routine they followed every morning. *"I am going for my usual breakfast, omelettes. What about you Harry?"* Harry nodded and as always Khush ordered the same for both.

A startling discovery

Khush got busy reading *Mumbai Mirror*, flipping the pages eagerly. *"One more article on marijuana smuggling, this time it's a serious one,"* he exclaimed.

"Why serious?" asked Harry.

"Marijuana sales in city funding Naxals," replied Khush, reading the headline.

Marijuana sales in city funding Naxals - An Article from Mumbai Mirror on 24th September 2017

"Holy cow! This is serious!" acknowledged Harry with a grim nod. *"This is getting very nasty indeed."* he said as Khush tilted the newspaper, and he craned his neck to see the article.

"So now our city is supporting the Naxals." he continued.

Finding a solution

"How do we stop that?" enquired Khush.

"What can we possibly do about it!" repeated Harry. *"The Government is responsible; they ought to do something about it."*

"They have been trying to do something about it for ages, without any success. What different would they possibly do now?" asked Khush.

"There is only one way to stop it," said Harry, "by legalising marijuana. In my days we called it Mary Jane, rope, ganja."

"Sure, like weed, grass and joy-stick, the list goes on and on. The multitude of names shows how popular it is. You just cannot eradicate the use. The pushers are here to stay, the way it was in the West. This clearly shows that you cannot stop people from consuming it. As a result, by banning it, you are facilitating smuggling, corruption and now, terrorism."

"As Tapan Ghosh once said; what is forbidden is most desirable. This is a fact of life," concluded Harry.

A hard look at ourselves

"First of all, we are very backward, like the Americans were in the bootlegging days. Gujarat and now Bihar are dry, what can we expect from this country." emphasized Khush.

"Ha, ha, so true! For that matter, we have restrictions on our food preferences too. Holy Cow!" added Harry.

"Holy Cow Indeed! Ha, ha, ha, that's a good one", agreed Khush.

"In the first place, why did the West ban marijuana, not tobacco?" Khush was furious. *"That's how the Italian mafia shook up the world."* Khush was charged up and Harry was amused to see him surfing the net on his iPhone frantically.

"Look," he said, *"according to the World Health Organisation (WHO), India is home to 12% of the world's smokers. In 2009, about 900,000 people died in India due to smoking. According to a 2002 WHO estimate, 30% of adult males in India smoke."*

Harry nodded vigorously in acknowledgment after reading the report.

"See this! From Indian Express," said Khush, pointing his iPhone in Harry's direction, *"One Indian dies every 96 minutes due to alcohol consumption."*

Harry nodded again, looking at the phone screen.

"This is not done just for India. It's an international overdose research data. It's a new century and we are still searching for an answer to an age-old question: How many people have died overdosing on weed? The short answer: zero!"

"That too, with overdose," said Khush confidently, *"just one joint works wonders."*

Taking a radical approach

Harry was all smiles as he thought of something witty.

"Har fikr ko dhuen mein beshak udao

Har dhuen ko lekin Shiv dhyan banao"

He continued as Khush tried to make sense of the couplet. *"In fact, this herb is a cure for many diseases and not addictive like cigarettes and liquor. There is however, one major problem. Since it can be grown at home almost free, it poses a major threat to all the tobacco and alcohol barons around the world. If legalised, production and sale of marijuana can be a major source of tax revenue. Furthermore, all the money the pushers make can easily go to the government."*

"Surely," agreed Khush, *"and what's more, in the US and other places we have vaporisers and THC in mid-pens-weed sold in the cleanest and the healthiest form. The tax revenue apart, this will provide healthy pleasure to the people."*

Do you want people to drink, get aggressive and beat up their wives, smoke and cause irretrievable damage to their health or smoke-up and be at peace (bindaas) with the world? It's for you to decide.

HE & I

He was a handsome fellow but with an unusual attitude. I did not know whether to pity him or envy him, as there was nothing in-between about him.

Having been raised in an orphanage, he learnt to be street smart at an early age. The combination of being ambitious and a dreamer paved the way for the realisation of many of his dreams. At the age of 14 he pulled himself out of the hell that passed off for an orphanage. This was a few years after independence.

The outside world was tough. He became a house-help, though he also had the ingenuity to make money as a black marketeer of movie tickets or as a pickpocket.

He always aspired to be in the company of the rich and famous. As a quick learner, he soon melded with his employers. He worked hard to please them and, in the process, he learnt their ways and their take on life. He befriended everyone, identified their weaknesses and was ever willing to do their dirty work. He was everyone's favourite.

I tried my best to probe him but to no avail. My years of experience in wellness and welfare of kids in orphanages was being threatened. One day I countered him and asked whether he was planning to steal from the house. He denied the charge.

I tried to reason with him. He worked hard, yet drew only a pittance. He could make four times as much even with clean and honourable work. He blocked my enquiry by asserting that he didn't need the money.

This was strange. I was not able to trust him; he was too much into himself. I consider myself a good judge of youngsters of his age. However, I was not able to gauge this boy. I remained alert to his moves. For the first time I began to doubt myself. But soon I diverted towards other things that demanded my attention and since I heard nothing adverse on this front, this boy took a back seat in my mind.

Almost a decade passed and one day, I was stupefied on seeing a familiar face staring at me. He was behind the wheels of a fancy car, a Kingsway Dodge at New Market.

The girl sitting next to him smiled and said something, expecting a reaction, which didn't materialise. He probably didn't want me to witness anything. She nudged him but did not get the desired reaction. She followed his eye. Seeing me watch her, she promptly left with a hurried 'bye'. I recognised her as the only daughter in the house he served; she had been a pretty girl at 11 years of age and now she looked a 'sweet sixteen'.

As soon as she left, he came up to me. I was eager to know what was going on between them. We got into the car and drove off. He showed off his sedan by telling me about its powerful 3.6-litre, 6-cylinder engine.

"So, you are a chauffeur now." I remarked.

"And a bodyguard, a facilitator and a confidant." he added.

"How much do you earn?"

"I get 500 as salary, plus commission and the profit from the distribution of litho tin boxes of State Express 555 cigarettes."

He offered me one and lit it with a fancy Zippo lighter he was drawing my attention to. I was impressed.

"500 is a handsome salary; the GM of Wesman Engineering gets only 800."

"My total income varies from 800 to 1500."

His claims were absurd I thought, as my gaze shifted from his sports jacket to the Daniel Wellington on his wrist. It was shocking. I was probably in the company of a bigtime criminal. He sensed my uneasiness and smiled. Was he the same kid from the orphanage? But how was that possible? The person beside me came across as a cultured young man, probably could claim that his roots belonged to a royal family. This was possible during the colonial era when Indian princesses fell in love with handsome officers with such bizarre results. I felt the urge to trace his ancestors, but everything had a cost attached to it.

Looking at me with concern, he said, *"I have not stolen this watch, Artelia presented it to me."*

"Who is Artelia?"

"Buck's wife."

And who is Buck?"

"He's a big man. Buck James Duke is the Chairman of Ardath Tobacco Company, which makes these cigarettes," he said, taking the stub out of his lips and chucking it out of the window as we drove to Victoria Memorial. *"Artelia must be his second wife; she is much younger than him. Buck insisted that I accept the gift. I used to bring her here often, to Victoria Memorial."*

"What did you do with her?"

"We enjoyed each other's company a lot."

"What about Buck? Didn't he object?"

"Not at all. He was grateful to have me as his wife's companion. He was busy impressing the Americans to sell his brand for markets outside the UK and Calcutta was his biggest market. I was his representative and hosted all his parties. Couples like Artelia and I would dance cheek to cheek with the dim lights and the smoke shielding us from any gaze."

He offered me another cigarette but I declined. He lit one stylishly.

Why do you smoke so much?

"This is from the time I was a kid. I used to clean ashtrays and collect the butts to smoke. I always had a longing for full ones."

I felt bad for him.

It was hard to believe the journey he had covered. But he was in front of me in flesh and blood. Just one look at him sitting behind the wheel said it all. He had royal blood in him without doubt. My curiosity got the better of me. I decided to grill him.

"I don't believe all that you are telling me. How do you expect me to believe that in 10 years' time you became a sahib from a ghulaam? How did that happen?"

"I don't know how but I had made up my mind when I was about five years old."

"What did you do?"

"I was sent to an Englishman Colonel Peter Fleming, whose eyes sparkled when he saw me. He was good to me and gave me things I had never been exposed to. He lovingly took off my clothes and led me to a luxurious bathroom with fancy toiletries. He bathed me and kissed me all over my body, slurping away and grunting at times. I felt ticklish.

"How dare he, the dirty old man! Why was I not told? Did he hurt you?"

"No, I realised much later he was not able to get hard enough to hurt me. He kept pressing me all over with his organ before ejaculating on me and getting away panting. I felt dirty. He poured water and soap and I cleaned myself while he dragged himself to the bed. Soon, he was snoring away. He later brought me new clothes. This is how I was brought up. I realised the weakness of these people and took advantage of it. I am now getting the reward for the torture I went through."

This is the reality! This is what we humans have done to ourselves. Here is a man who can speak out because he has conquered himself; others live with their miseries buttoned up inside them. Some become hardened criminals. I couldn't help but sympathise with him.

"My God, I cannot imagine the experiences you have gone through."

"I was lucky. People go through much more."

"You seem to have no regrets."

He looked confused and immersed in his thoughts. I could not fathom him. I did not know what to make out of the guy. He always seemed to be in a good mood, with no self-pity.

"...I was his front man to distribute tins of 555 to all the guests awaiting the arrival of the big American..."

"Please stop; the tram is approaching, I must go. It was nice talking to you. I am sure you know where to find me. It's the same place in Ballygunge you came to, before this job."

"I will certainly do so, thank you."

"Look after yourself. God bless!"

I did not know what to make out of this conversation. He gave the impression of not knowing what he was up to, nor did he care since he adapted to everything that came his way. He went with the flow; with whatever was in store for him.

OF MONKEYS AND MEN

"We have indeed descended from monkeys as we too are copycats."

Have you heard of a man being stopped in his tracks by a giant monkey? What I am about to narrate is no story or figment of imagination. It *actually* happened to me.

It was in the middle of nowhere that I encountered a strange and seemingly dangerous situation that made me question our pre-conditioned thinking. Why do we respond to situations in a certain set fashion? Is it because we have been told to unquestioningly judge right and wrong based on certain ambiguous parameters? Do our instincts turn to insecurities? Do they create distances between us and others, rather than cocoon us from the unknown? Here's an incident that triggered these questions.

25 km from Rishikesh, the *Vashistha Cave* is named after Rishi Vashistha, guru of Lord Rama and *manasputra* (human progeny) of Lord Brahma. One of the *saptarishis* (seven great sages) of ancient times, it is believed that Vashistha meditated and lived here till the age of 85 when he attained nirvana.

Having visited the cave, I was walking down the path that connected it with the approach road. The vibrations I had felt there – coupled with the serene environment – had a calming effect on me. Lost in thought, I didn't realise that a giant monkey had positioned itself further ahead, blocking my path, until we were a couple of feet apart. A sense of panic gripped me. I froze, fearing that any movement on my part might antagonize it. An eerie silence enveloped us.

Getting into an impasse

"We keep away from monkeys because they represent the real us whom we refuse to acknowledge."

For what seemed a long time, there was no movement on either side. It was a tense situation. I had to get away but running wasn't an option. Worse, any movement on my part evoked a similar response from the ape. We had reached an impasse.

Several agonizing moments later, I started all over again, I took two tentative steps, only to see the monkey match my action. But the dilemma had been broken. The mind and body were in synch again. I took another step and the monkey did the same.

As I kept going, I could see the monkey keep pace with me. Our movements seemed to be synchronised. The mind was racing with several thoughts. What must I do next? How should I shake him off my trail? I started walking towards the main road, he alongside, a bit concerned as this was not his regular beat. I felt slightly relieved that I had managed to make it this far without aggravating the primate.

An unexpected call

"Only those who love themselves will love monkeys as pets."

But my problems weren't over yet. Suddenly the phone in my pocket began to ring. I quickly turned it off as I saw him getting worked up, teeth bared, screeching shrilly, all poised to attack. It was scary. The renewed silence calmed him down and we continued our synchronized walk.

My mind was busy, planning an escape out of this strained situation. We were now in safer territory, but there were no people close by. A few in the distance were too far to call out to, without running the risk of agitating my walking partner. I shook my head at my helplessness. He shook his head too, seemingly in mock concern.

Relief at hand

"Aren't we monkeys at heart? Don't we like to monkey around? Each one of us has an alter ego that keeps monkeying around."

Suddenly, my car arrived. I figured that it must have been the driver who had called a few moments earlier. My friend was startled.. I quietly went ahead, opened the rear door and with a wave of my hand, signaled him to join me in the car. I almost broke out into laughter as he did the same. Confrontation had given way to courtesy. Pushing my luck, I extended the invitation one more time. After you, he gestured. Seizing the opportunity, I jumped into the car and slammed the door shut before he could follow me. The driver shot off immediately.

From the safety of the moving vehicle, I turned back to see a puzzled look on the monkey's face. Strangely, I wanted to go back. Picking up a stem of bananas from a vendor down the road, we returned to the spot where we had left him. He was still there.

Clearing the misunderstanding

"We often talk about mind over matter, not realising that sometimes it is the monkey in us over mind."

I stepped out of the car and walked towards him. Puzzled at my hasty exit, the monkey followed my every move. Our eyes were now locked in contact. I walked as close to him as my instinct would permit. Placing the bunch of fruit on the edge of the road, I waved my arm, inviting him to partake of the feast. He didn't budge an inch. His eyes were still locked on mine.

I was no longer afraid. Turning away, I calmly walked back to the car. As we drove away, I turned around to see the monkey approach the pile of bananas. He pulled one off the stem, unpeeled it and bit into it. He looked pleased as he relished the first bite. Perhaps he now realized that I wasn't a foe after all.

I felt a sense of relief too. Our initial confrontation had turned into an unspoken understanding. Our own insecurities prevent us from understanding others, be it humans or other creatures. I came away feeling that we might be able to understand other people better if we attempt to understand animals first.

This was my first major interaction with a monkey and thereafter, there have been some chance meetings. Once, when two tiny monkeys entered my window after ransacking my neighbour's house, I remained calm and was prepared for them. They just looked at me and quietly went back the way they had come from.

By and large I have noticed people are scared of monkeys as they're quite unstable and difficult to predict. We may identify with dogs, but not with monkeys. This is because we do not want to identify with monkeys. We don't want to face the truth that we have evolved from them.

"We do not tolerate any monkey business because we dare not revel ourselves. We hate monkeys. They are so unstable. Bloody copycats!"

UNDERSTANDING ATTACHMENT

Attachment is the biggest curse of life.

All our problems emanate from it. Self-attachment is nothing but ego, the deadliest of all attachments, which results in enslavement to power and wealth - the fundamental cause of all insecurity.

Attachment is difficult to get rid of, because it is like sticky tape. When you try to detach yourself from a person or thing, attachment binds you to someone or something else. Detachment is a gradual process. A forcible attempt at it is mere suppression of attachment, with the risk of attachment rebounding stronger than before.

Nature provides several examples of this phenomenon. The use of insecticides increases the immunity of insects, making them deadlier than before. Likewise, antibiotics administered to suppress disease lose their potency after a while. Tobacco addicts who quit smoking abruptly often get back to it with a vengeance. Or worse, they over-eat to satiate the desire suppressed by smoking. This often results in bingeing, leading to obesity.

Doctors must teach, rather than treat. Build immunity not through antibiotics and vitamins but by healthy living.

Attachment in a relationship is the ultimate challenge life can impose. It can make one very possessive and insecure. This often has repercussions that may be difficult to control or overcome. The insecurities of the mind assume control over the heart.

Worldly pressures often destroy the purity of love and lead to breakups. Fortunately, breakups can also be a solution, if done not against one another but with each other. By working as a team to gradually make one independent of the other. This is difficult and trying, and demands a disciplined mind and complete faith. The gradual process will keep the love alive as the process of detaching from one another unfolds.

Salvation is nothing but attaining the golden mean between the mind and the heart. It does away with the negativity in either, and leaves behind love, faith and discipline. Faith brings positivity, which makes the disciplined mind detach from the insecurities that consume most of your energy. This energy can be used for growth of character. This is nothing but elevating your physical, mental, emotional and spiritual self. You rise in love. This is the freedom we yearn for, of which happiness is a by-product.

Everything done with belief is wise, not otherwise / A relationship is a cause of interdependence likewise.

A GORGEOUS PARSI WIDOW IN WILD GOA

What do you do when you are young, beautiful, sexy and condemned to the lonely life of a widow? Especially in a wild and gorgeous place like Goa! Can family restrictions hold you down when your hormones are running wild?

Hey, I can see what you are up to!

Gorgeous Goa has always been notorious for being a 'swinging' place. The atmosphere is such that everyone is in the mood for adventure and fun. One of the quieter parts of the territory had a Parsi neighbourhood. The neighbours usually kept to themselves. Two of the houses here were located in such close proximity that living in one, you could see what was going on in the other.

Mere samne waali khidki mein ik chand ka tukda rehta hai / A moon-like beauty lives in the house facing mine!

An elderly couple lived in each of the two houses. However, one of houses had a sexy young widowed daughter-in-law living with her in-laws. Such was her charm that both men – her father-in-law and the neighbour – had the hots for her. The neighbour used to describe her as *"umar ma moti pan ekdam juvaan ne dudh jevi gori chatak!"* The neighbour's study faced the widow's room and he spent a lot of time eyeing her after turning off the lights in that room at night. Of course, he used to lie to his wife about wanting to read in the study, so as not to disturb her sleeping in their bedroom.

Given the somewhat remote location of the neighbourhood in an otherwise swinging Goa, the widow was desperate for some action but was caught between two lame ducks. Until one day when the neighbour's grandson came down from the US to visit his grandparents for the first time. Having lived all his adult life in the US, he was not conversant with the Indian way of life.

Saamne ye kaun aaya, dil mein hui halchal / Who have I come across, my heart throbs with excitement!

One afternoon, while exploring the nearby market, he came across a beautiful young woman who seemed to be having trouble starting her scooter.

Seeing her concern, he offered to help and soon got the scooter working. The woman – who was the captivating widow – was relieved and offered to drop him to his destination. He looked attractive and both seemed to enjoy talking to each other. Parsis being a small community, they discovered that the boy had, in fact, lived in her neighbourhood as a ten-year old. He even remembered having attended her wedding to a naval officer about 20 years earlier. The widow told him that her husband had died in the last war with Pakistan.

She offered to drop him home and was thrilled to find out that they were neighbours once again. They kept chatting long after reaching the Parsi neighbourhood. Seated in the study, the grandfather remarked, *"Hoosna pari jevi chhokri, my boy!"*

Husn ke laakhon rang, kaunsa rang dekhoge? / Beauty holds a million charms, what's the one that appeals to you?

Late in the night, when the entire neighbourhood was asleep, the sexy widow put on a teeny-weeny negligee with all the lights in her room on. Dancing provocatively to music playing on her system, she caught the attention of the boy who was in his grandfather's study. Totally charged, the boy ran out of his house and rushed towards the neighbouring house, entering it through the toilet window. She was waiting for him. *"Chhelle tu aavi j gayo!"* Grabbing him by his shirt, she dragged him to the room and pushed him down to the bed. She ripped off his shirt and put off the lights as they got entangled in bed.

Moaning with pleasure, she climaxed with a wild scream. It was so loud that perhaps half the neighbourhood heard it. The in-laws in the next room woke up with a start. They called out to her and rushed to her room. The widow froze as she realised this. Shaking the boy off, she screamed 'rape, rape.' The boy bolted. She opened the door and her father-in-law barged in, trying to balance his shotgun. *"Kon gadhedo andar ghusi gayo chhe?"*

Chal uddja re panchi, ye des hua begaana / Time to move on, buddy. There's nothing going for you here!

The woman pointed to the toilet between sobs. The father-in-law cautiously entered the toilet with his trembling hands on the shotgun. *"Kya bharai gayo? Baar nikad!"* Finding no one there, he swore, *"Bhaagi gyo, saalo."* *"Bhastegiya! Taroo nakhhod jay!"* he said. At that moment, the boy entered his house to an unexpected surprise; holding a camera in his hand, his grandpa was laughing away.

Seeing an apprehensive look on the boy's face, the grandfather said, *"Khali chano j jorthi vaage. What's that lame duck going to do with his shotgun? You and I are the only shooters here. You, with your tool and I, with mine,"* he said, holding up his camera. Laughing again in response to the boy's inquiring look, he added, *"There is no need to worry. There was no rape. I have all the evidence here till the lights went off. You know the rest."* The grandson smiled mischievously.

Everyone in the story acted according to their point of view. The young widow felt the need for companionship that was denied by social norms. The boy's liberal upbringing in the US made him act in a way that would not be frowned upon in that country. The widow's father-in-law was only trying to protect her, as was expected of him. The boy's grandfather was exploiting the opportunity of being so close to his neighbour. Did anyone act out of character? What do you think?

UNFAIR AND UN-LOVELY!

Khush: *You have always talked about the white-skin complex in our country. Look at this article I just read — how we Indians are crazy about the whites. We keep hankering for selfies with them. This is so humiliating!*

Harry: *You can say this again. This complex is a major reason for the downfall of our country. I have personally suffered a lot in my career, from the very onset. I am sure there are a million others who suffer every day.*

Khush: *Really! How come you have never told me this? What happened? Was it really bad?*

Harry: *Indeed! A do-or-die situation. I had no option but to cheat.*

Khush: *Cheat? Oh! You mean the Anglo-Indian Bollywood actor you used to impersonate as an engineering expert? Ah yes, you told me this a long time ago. What was his name?*

Harry: *Steven Kingsley. It was fun to make him do all that.*

Khush: *You didn't do all that for fun, did you?*

Harry: *No! My entire purchase order for critical equipment would have been cancelled had I not got a white-skin expert from my licensor to be at the factory during the manufacturing stage.*

Khush: *Why?*

Harry: *I could neither afford nor convince the licensor to send someone from their office every week. That left me with no option but to hire an Anglo-Indian actor as a substitute.*

Khush: *Oh really! What could the actor have done? He had no knowledge of your field.*

Harry: *He just had to do his job. That was to act and I had to direct him.*

Khush: *This is really funny. What did you ask him to do?*

Harry: *I told him to speak in an accent no one understood and I acted as the translator. He had to say 'no' whenever I raised my eyebrow, 'yes' otherwise. He was a good actor and I, a good script writer.*

Khush: *And how did you convince the client?*

Harry: *With a white-skin holder of a British passport by my side, my work progressed speedily and without the usual interference and inspection. However, getting a letter from the licensor stating that the actor was their expert needed some doing. It had to be done as both of us would have lost money had the order been cancelled.*

Khush: *What about the equipment? Did everything work out well? Your expertise is well-known; you couldn't have failed.*

Harry: *Where was the question of failing? The equipment has been working flawlessly for the past 20 years. The tragedy is that we Indians don't trust ourselves. We need a white-skin licensor to endorse what we do. Despite having talented engineers, it's a shame that we continue to import technology.*

Khush: *Sad!*

Harry: *Yes. I had to tie-up with this licensor for five years. And pay them 7% for merely endorsing every piece of equipment I made using technology I had developed.*

Khush: *My God! What a loss to the nation! Why do we have this complex?*

Harry: *Ask yourself, Khushroo Screwvala! Didn't you fair-skinned Parsis sucked up to the British rulers who were much lighter-complexioned?*

Khush: *Rascal, how dare you? On what grounds did you say that?*

Harry: *I am just stating a fact. How else can the Parsis push their way around in India so well but fail in the West?*

Khush: *You bastard! You are a turncoat. You are saying that we're responsible for India's downfall?*

Harry: *Not at all. On the contrary you guys have done a lot of good for the country in every field.*

Khush: *Then who are you blaming, you rouge?*

Harry: *This is not a blame game, just a fallout of the British rule in India. Since there weren't enough Englishwomen here, they married the locals and gave rise to the Anglo-Indian community. This community turned out to be more British in their ways then the British themselves. They were given key positions in every field on account of their light-colour skin. This is how the white-skin complex spread in our country.*

Khush: *I see your point now. How do we eradicate it?*

Harry: *On the contrary, the complex has only become more deeply entrenched post-independence. We are increasingly dependent on them for technology. Every company ties up with a foreign brand. We even hire white-skin staff to market our products in India. The heads of departments are white because it is believed that they will be able to control the non-whites better.*

Khush: *Now, that's going too far. Why don't we understand this?*

Harry: *We need to make people aware of this fact. And repose confidence in the abilities of our fellow countrymen. Many Indians are heading corporations abroad. Proof enough that we Indians are in no way inferior to others.*

DOGS CAN SMELL A RAT

As a kid, I too dreamt of having a dog, like many do. But I was denied that joy when I brought home a neighbour's pup. My mother refused to have him. It would be either her or the dog. My dad asked me to look after myself first before I tried taking responsibility of another creature. I realised that they were right.

Later in life when I graduated in engineering, I set up a factory on a one-acre plot in TTC MIDC to manufacture heat exchangers. I needed a watch dog for the premises but wondered how to get one. I was lucky. I got a dog whose master had just expired and there was no one to look after him. A big, strong, three-year old, male German Shepherd; the dog of my dreams.

All that I knew about dogs was from books. This guy gave me a tough time. Although he was put on a leash, he was too ferocious for anyone to approach him, even to place milk or food within his reach. The moment I would approach him, he would leap, bark and growl with his teeth showing. He was protesting for being tied up.

I decided to give him a bath with a hosepipe. He objected so ferociously that the metal gate he was chained to, began to rattle. Wanting to tame him, I increased the water pressure and pointed the hose towards his face. He kept moving out of the line and I kept aligning it in line with his face. We set a frantic pace. Moving from left to right and back in a matter of seconds with a high-pressure hose was tiring but neither of us would budge. Just as I was about to give up, he did and settled down with a whimper.

Both of us were panting away; he with his long tongue hanging. I could now go near him and untie the chain. He accepted me and we went on a long walk. When we returned, he was sniffing away as delicious meat was waiting for him in a big bowl. He quickly gulped it down. I was his new master and he was my best friend.

I called him Boozo and we got along so well with each other. He was a well-trained dog. Both of us would often go for a long walk and climb the nearby hills. I loved to show off Boozo, especially when the two of us juggled with a football. It used to be quite a sight, much to the amusement of people around. Playing with him was a good workout for me. There were times he would get past me and at other times I would dribble better. His head against my bare feet on the grass.

I once had a friend over for dinner and a rat scurried past us while we were eating. My friend chased the rat but it hid itself behind a steel cupboard placed against a wall.

"I will need Boozo's help," I said. My friend laughed when I called out to Boozo. *"How can he hear you when he is at the other end of the plot?"* he enquired.

The next moment - even to my surprise -the fellow was there, panting away with his long tongue hanging out. I pointed to the cupboard. Boozo could smell a rat. He hit the cupboard with his powerful paws and the rat rushed out from the left. But Boozo was faster. He slapped the rat with his paw and the rat was done. Boozo looked up at me, pride evident on his face. I gave him a smile, pointed to the dead rat and called out his name as a command. He picked up the rat and walked off. My friend looked aghast!

Humans love dogs and like to teach them like we teach babies. However, we have a lot to learn from dogs. The question is, how do we learn from them when we judge them wrongly?

Dogs live for the moment and die only once, whereas we die every moment. If we only learn to stretch like dogs when we get up from sleep, the blood circulating through our body will give us a high bigger than we get from drinking a cup of coffee.

Dogs are the animals closest to us. No wonder we use words like 'dog' and a 'bitch' to describe people. Human beings have double standards, dogs don't. How misplaced is our perception, when we think of ourselves as being superior! We use a derogatory term to call others a dog or a bitch, not realising that there is no relationship purer than the one between a dog and a bitch.

Every man is a dog, and every woman, a bitch. Like a dog, man has a tendency to sniff around and like a bitch, women like to assume control.

Our world is a dog-eat-dog world. Not for the dogs, because dogs don't believe in the world. Unlike us, they only believe in themselves.

SHE AND HE

She could be very demanding at times. A rare occurrence though, only in the privacy of her dear ones, whose love she took for granted. Her upbringing was the reason for such behaviour. A giver at heart, who slaved for everyone, she loved to be acknowledged in return. Those who knew about her deprived childhood understood what she sought.

As a child, she often saw her dad beat up and abuse her mom for compromising his dignity with the birth of a girl child.

When, at last, a boy was born, the father was perpetually on an ego trip with his drunken friends. This was a never-ending embarrassment at home with drunkards eyeing the women. The man of the house did not care two hoots about anyone but himself. He was forever flexing his muscles or whatever was left of them, with his health and wealth diminishing by the day. The fair-weather friends would now leave early, with the man of the house bedridden and no alcohol to drink. The sick man could barely down his medicines.

One night a friend came back to the house quite drunk and went straight to the kitchen. The girl at once realised that he was the one who eyed her mother. She feigned ignorance but remained alert. Before she could warn her mother, who was busy cooking, he made a pass at her mother. The mother hastily stepped back warning him. He drew close and pressed her body against his. Before he could do anything further, a sharp knife pierced his buttocks. The house was full of screams and there was blood all over the kitchen floor. The girl ran out in panic.

The rapist ended up in police custody and the girl at her loving grandmother's house, a short distance away from hers. The man died of cirrhosis of the liver, leaving behind debts and ill fame. She was only fourteen, her mother thirty-four, and her brother, a six-year-old brat.

With the mother looking after the house and the brother schooling, the girl became the sole bread-earner of the family. From the age of twelve, she and her mom had run the family's tailoring business, which had flourished while her *Nana* was alive. All this had to be subsequently sold off to clear their debts.

The girl now took up a job as an assistant to a reputed physiotherapist and was soon promoted as her deputy. She learnt to manipulate the joints. She was gradually introduced to rich men needing treatment or a massage, whatever it may be called. *Masseuse* is not a polite word for a lucrative carrier, and so, they are called massage therapists. She worked at the wellness centre for the mind, body and soul. What happens within the four walls and on the massage bed depends on how the customer and the therapist meld with each other.

She was a sincere worker and everyone's favourite, but giving in to customers' demands was not an option. The only exception was for him, she and he were one. He was the only stabilising feature in her life apart from grandma. They would massage each other and stretch each other's bodies in all the yogic postures and more.

She put his endurance to the test. In the most awkward position she preferred, he went on. He accomplished a lot more as he knew that no one else could satiate her appetite. He considered this as a God-given opportunity to salvage her needs as they manifested. He thought his neck would break, his jaws would freeze, or his tongue would come apart. Why should he not be able to bear this pain?

The rewards took long, but they came at last. He felt her fingers on his head lovingly caressing his hair, her legs gripping his back, enclosing him, and finally, her heels rubbing against his back vigorously till culmination. They were in bliss and watching her gave him a high. The spontaneous joy of the recipient is the giver's highest experience of purity. He was a giver more than she could fathom, the others who visited her were just takers. A masochist is a true giver whose endurance can satisfy even the most demanding.

She was in love with his ways, a dream come true for her, as he loved to fulfill all her demands. She took his love for granted. The best part was that he made no demands on her as if he had no needs. The others were just the opposite. He was God-sent indeed, a reward for all her sufferings. She could tell him her mind. They let down their guard and they could see through each other. The only obstacle was the language, as her education was limited to primary school. However, her street-smartness and wisdom made up for it. As a massage therapist, she knew how to service both body and mind. Her employer and her clients would seek her opinion on important matters.

He could not be termed a client although he was generous with money and he came to her for reasons beyond imagination. The only explanation for his peculiar behaviour was that, unlike a sadist, a masochist like him catered to the partner's demand instead of making them.

It was a unique situation and she felt blessed. But for this, there would have been no respite and nothing for her to look forward to in life. He, on the other hand, would experience the highest purity from the spontaneous joy she demonstrated as a reaction to his actions. He firmly believed that sex was all about fulfilling the needs of the recipient. Real men are givers who serve a demanding woman to evaluate their endurance.

WILL ROBOTS BE A THREAT TO SOCIETY?

Khush: *Are robots going to be a threat to society?*

Harry: *Which society?*

Khush: *What do you mean?*

Harry: *Our society or theirs?*

Khush: *What? Their society? What are we talking about?*

Harry: *Don't you know?*

Khush: *Don't I know what?*

Harry: *Are you going to only ask questions?*

Khush: *Aa ha, now I know, you are just pulling my leg. No more questions. I am just worried about what I read in the papers.*

Harry is amused when Khush shows him the article in *The Times of India* titled *Skin with Sense of Touch Created for Robots.*

Harry: *Ha ha, this will worry brothel owners around the world.*

Khush: *Why them?*

Harry: *Because of Fanny – a brothel's £72-an-hour sex doll. It has been such a hit with clients that it has become more popular than real prostitutes. It is often completely booked for several days in a row. This is what The Mirror, UK reports.*

Khush: *Wow! Now they are going to be sensual too.*

Harry: *Yes. Moreover, with artificial intelligence taking the lead, robots are going to replace your friends as they will be programmed to do as you please, without getting under your skin like humans do.*

Khush: *Holy crap! We don't know what can happen in times to come.*

Harry: *We don't have a choice. 24/7 attention with zero hang ups is too tempting to resist.*

Khush: *Is this really possible?*

Harry: *Of course! It is a bit futuristic that's all. It's already making business sense.*

Khush: *It may not, as they will not be affordable.*

Harry: *Just wait and watch! Leave it to the Chinese to make it affordable, give them some time to get over their teething problems.*

Khush: *My God! What if you are right? It would be hell. How did this come upon us?*

Harry: *How? Greed, insecurity, fear! We've done this to ourselves. For centuries we have fought to prove that we are the best, our religion is the only true one. In the name of God, we have committed the biggest immoral acts. Moral, ethics and the code of conduct have been created by those who are insecure. These are the people who impose their dos and don'ts upon us.*

Khush: *We have already suffered by going against the laws of nature. And now the robots! What do we do? Did you really mean they will have their own society when you asked which society I was talking about?*

Harry: *Yes! They will have a society of their own. Their language is different as they follow the binary code. Facebook conducted experiments on artificial intelligence where they made two robots talk to each other. Shockingly, the robots took over and the researchers couldn't understand the conversation. They were not in control. They panicked and switched off the button.*

Khush: *Horrifying! You are right, our greed has no limits. Once we create them, they could assume control. That will be a major threat.*

Harry: *Yes! To all the smart people.*

Khush: *What do you mean?*

Harry: *The crafty ones. No one can be smarter or more efficient than robots. Only the arty ones will survive. Art demands original thinking.*

Khush: *The arty ones in India have been rotting. They live in a world of their own and are considered fools.*

Harry: *A fool does not know that he is a fool simply because he is not one. We are! It is an irony that the people of this country so rich in spirituality are now just imitating the West. On the other hand, having discovered our spiritual capacity, the West is adopting our culture.*

Khush: *Very true! So, what do we do?*

Harry: *Nothing. We have spiritual energy, which helps understand the world and its problems, the sufferings and the craftiness. On the one hand we are victims of peer pressure while on the other, we know the purity of truth. If we believe in ourselves, no robot can conquer our faith.*

Neither man, nor machine can replace its creator.

IS THE WORLD GOING POTTY?

As always, Khush and Harry were enjoying omelettes and coffee after a game of tennis. Khush was reading the Times of India, his favourite newspaper. A particular article caught his attention and he excitedly thrust the newspaper in Harry's direction.

Khush: *Hey look! Someone has written an article relating to the scene you created in a five-star hotel in Delhi some time ago. That must have spread like wildfire.*

Harry: *About the toilets, you mean. Thank God someone has had the guts to write about it. I gave my secretary a firing for messing up that time. I don't care about being booked in a 4-star hotel or 5-star, but I must have a jet spray after I take a crap. This one didn't. Most of the big hotel chains don't."*

Khush looked amused as he kept reading more.

Khush: *It sure is a well-written article. Has this writer heard you talk? He mentions the issue exactly the way you describe it. According to him, toilet paper doesn't clean properly. It leaves traces which can cause infection. Also, toilet paper can damage the skin which is particularly sensitive down there. The Indian way of using water to clean up is the most appropriate.*

Harry: *We Indians are more hygienic than the rest of the world in our toilet habits. And all of us face this problem in star hotels.*

Khush: *What do you do when you're stuck in a 5-star abroad?*

Harry: *I manage somehow in the ones that have a bidet. But the one in Delhi did not even have that, so I lost my cool.*

Khush: *What do you do in such situations?*

Harry: *You want to know the gory details, don't you? Well, I plan it well by keeping two wet tissues ready, so that I don't have to get up from the seat.*

Khush: *I see! What should we Indians do to educate the world?*

Harry: *Firstly, it's high time we stopped aping the West blindly. And the world must be educated about the ill-effects of using toilet paper. Hygiene apart, imagine the damage to the environment caused by cutting millions of trees every year for toilet paper! Not to mention the millions of tonnes of waste generated every year – this can easily be avoided by using water instead.*

Khush: *Indeed!*

Harry: *How many people know that we Indians of the Indus Valley Civilisation (Mohenjo-Daro) were the first to invent a flush toilet 5000 years ago?*

Khush: *Wow! That's great. Then why are we so backward?*

Harry: *Because we're lazy, not the industrious sort. We're just arty, not crafty like the West. I must give credit to the Americans for the work culture they have developed. We lack that attitude.*

SALVATION IN LOVE: RENDEZVOUS AT THE CAFE

There was a couple sitting in the cafe when I walked in. As the light was low, I didn't know who they were until the woman turned around, and I saw it was my wife. Oh! They are already here. Shobha is always a step ahead, I thought, as I pitched myself forward from behind the pillar.

"Hey Sanjeev! Why is this place so dark and gloomy? You look different in the dark, but I could recognise Shobha even in the dark," I said.

"You better! Why are you so late?" she enquired.

"I'm not, you're early as usual. I almost went back thinking that you guys would be on the other side of the mall. Luckily, I spotted you," I replied.

"Sanjeev is nervous because Anusha is expected any moment," she said.

He was not just worried, he was tensed. I put my hand on his shoulder to calm him down a bit and said.

"Don't worry Sanjeev, we'll handle her."

"We shouldn't have called her, she's not going to like, what we tell her." screamed Sanjeev, clearly jittery.

"I have got her number, I'll call her to ease her off," I replied but Sanjeev snatched the phone from my hand.

"She doesn't even know you," he said.

I couldn't control my laughter at his comment.

"What are you laughing about? I have never done this before, I'm nervous."

"He's right. Stop making fun of him, Harry," said Shobha, giving me a stern look.

"Okay, count me out. I won't call her, you guys do what you think is right, I'll leave."

"No, please don't, I'm sorry. What will you tell her?" asked Shobha.

I was about to answer when we saw Anusha looking for us. Sanjeev was startled to see her. His expression revealed that he wanted me to back him in the situation.

"Okay, I am here. Tell me why I have been called," she asked.

Not getting a response from Sanjeev, she moved her gaze towards Shobha, trying to start a conversation.

"Hi Shobha, what's cooking? I haven't seen you in a long time. Fortunately, my teeth are in good condition. What have you done to my husband's teeth?" she enquired.

"He has sensitive teeth," replied Shobha awkwardly, waiting for me to take over.

"I see! Is that why he is at your clinic all day? Don't you have other patients or are you as out of work as he is?" charged Anusha.

"I am not jobless; I have a flourishing practice."

"How are you allowed to operate from your residence?"

"The same way as you do."

"I am only running a consultancy, working on my computer. But you are running a practice that needs a lot of room and equipment."

"My husband has given me two flats renovated into one with a separate entrance for the clinic. I extracted your wisdom tooth, which explains why you don't have any left," shot back Shobha.

Anusha lost her cool. *"Please keep your wisecracks to yourself. Just tell me, which bedroom is Sanjeev in, when you are with another patient?"*

Shobha was shocked as Anita moved towards her in a fury.

(To be continued…)

SALVATION IN LOVE: A 15-YEAR WAIT

I thought she was going a bit too far now and decided to intervene. Signalling Shobha to hold her horses, I stood in front of Anusha.

"Wait a minute, we are here for a purpose, not to argue," I said.

Anusha came charging towards me but with an intriguing smile unseen by the other two, as she had her back to them. I encouraged her with a wink that brought the smile back but no change in her tone when she questioned me.

"May I know how you are connected with the two of them?"

"Shobha is my wife," I said curtly and turned away, without showing much concern. I had put the ball back in Anusha's court for her to play the lead. She was quick on the take.

"What! What is this supposed to mean? Why am I here?"

She looked sharply at Sanjeev; he appeared to be completely shaken up. Shobha looked concerned about him and she glared at me angrily before getting up to speak. But Anusha told her to keep out of it by raising her hand and glaring at her accusingly.

Lest they come to blows, I decided to intervene. *"Stop it, both of you, this is a public place, no more of this talk, please,"* I said aloud.

Anusha stormed out of the cafe in a fury, throwing the ball back in my court. Thereby telling me, that she had fulfilled her role and it was now for me to conclude as I was supposed to.

"Stop her, stop her," screamed Sanjeev getting up and begging me to run after her.

I cajoled him to relax, as now it was my responsibility and Shobha did the rest of the convincing.

"She'll throw me out of the house, please help, where will I go?" he pleaded.

"If that happens, we'll put a door between my two flats. You and Shobha will live in the one with the clinic, and I in the other."

"Really! Are you sure?" His eyes were joyously sparkling and so were Shobha's.

"I promise! Shobha knows I never fail to keep my promises." I went in peace as I saw him looking at Shobha for confirmation which was affirmed with a nod, followed by a passionate hug.

Thank God, everything was going as per plan. It had taken me 15 years to set this up. I did not ditch Anusha when she was only 20 years old. I left her because I was not worthy of her. When I called her after a gap of 15 years, she was shocked and I heard her phone drop as it hit the ground.

She refused to meet me, but I kept trying to tell her that I had our best interest in mind. *"For what?"* she'd interrupt, *"for ditching me?"*

How reassuring it was when she remarked, a few days ago, that I looked fitter and younger than before. I now have all, I ever wanted, including my sweetheart. Was I taking things for granted? Yes, very much so.

Whenever you feel that you are in control of your life, the rug is pulled from beneath your feet, to keep you in control. It is the law of nature and this is what happened to me.

Anusha was nowhere to be found, not even at the other side of the mall, where we had decided to meet.

(To be continued…)

SALVATION IN LOVE: ALL'S WELL THAT ENDS WELL

The cafe was brightly lit by the sun shining through the glass. But I was missing the shining glow of my beloved. I tried to call her, but her phone was not reachable.

What could have gone wrong, I wondered? Why did she play her role so well if she was not in agreement? Definitely not just to oblige, but to know the facts that were now seen, as clear as glass.

Then why is she not pleased with the outcome? I thought she would be thrilled, but that was my mistake, you can't take things for granted and definitely not with a woman. They have their own perceptions. Let's live with them, I thought, as I saw her emerging from the restroom. I was relieved that at least she did not vanish leaving me in a lurch.

"Hi," I said aloud to draw her attention and she looked at me but seemed to be bugged about something. I decided not to react and so she did instead, to my continued silence.

"Your wife is a bitch! She has grabbed my husband too."

"That's not true, all that happened is my doing. I am the bastard who did everything to get you back."

"You just want to protect her because you're under her spell."

"Okay, if that's what you think, what do you want to do now?"

"I want her to keep away from my husband, I am prepared to mother him and make him mine. I don't want to lose a second battle against that slimy creature."

"Okay, done. I will not allow Sanjeev to enter my house and I will shift to another residence as soon as I can. I will also change Shobha and my phone numbers so that we are not accessible to either of you. I suggest you two do the same. Let's be confined to our own lives."

I said this with all my love and concern and ignoring all the venom she had poured out against Shobha. She was taken aback with my complete surrender to her cause. She started doubting her motives and for the first time, looked exhausted. I requested her to join me for a cup of coffee before we departed which she readily accepted. We entered the cafe. This place had positive vibes and was quite vibrant. Coffee was served unlike in other coffee shops. Anusha's mood was also turning positive. Being much younger than Shobha and I, she had more to learn about life. Only when you accept life, are you in control.

"Can I ask you something?" she said.

"Please do."

"How can you tolerate your wife's dalliance? She is so open about it."

"My wife is a confirmed cougar, better off mothering someone like Sanjeev, who needs it for his survival. They make a loving couple."

"What! How can you even think like that, he is my husband?"

"Forget about relationships, they're man-made. Do you love him?"

"How dare you talk about love, after what you've done to me?"

"Yes, not to you alone, I had to crucify my heart too, you know all that happened."

"All that happened to me, after you dumped me for Shobha."

"I did not dump you. Marriage is a social obligation and not made in heaven."

"This talk makes no sense now. What do you want from me? After 15 years you just call me up one day, do you take me for a call girl?

"No! You are my angel, these 15 years are finally over today, the 19th of August! I have kept track of every single day, as a prisoner would."

"Oh really! How do I believe you, a twenty-year-old was not kissed even once?"

"I had no right to raise your hopes as our marriage was an impossibility."

"Why?"

"How could we marry when I was 15 years your senior and a pauper who had to get his sister married first? Your rich dad would have killed us or committed suicide."

"But I loved you and we have lost 15 years of our lives."

"Romeo-Juliet sacrificed their entire life for the sake of love. We just

detached ourselves for the sake of love. Over the years, our devotion has deepened than ever. No one can take it away. It's your love that motivated me to prosper and become healthier."

"What will Shobha think when she knows about all this?"

"Shobha already knows. And please trust me, she has helped me through all my longings and attachments for you. Love is not about possession. Our love is causeless."

"I now feel the same way, do you think we should get married?"

"No love is not about relationships. We can be together whenever we feel like. I will put a door between my apartments. Shobha will live in the one with clinic and I in the other one, where you can move in."

"Will Shobha mind this?"

"No, and not only that, she'll be thrilled if I tell her that you have agreed to live with me. She is dying to be with Sanjeev. This arrangement is God's gift to all of us for our sacrifices, it's a win-win for all."

She put her hands in mine and her eyes turned moist, as I raised her hands to my lips. We were both longing for our first physical encounter, the most intense side of love.

IS TAPAN GHOSH OUT OF HIS MIND?

"When character is lost, nothing is lost; when wealth is lost, something is lost; but when health is lost, everything is lost." - Tapan Ghosh

"*Is Tapan Ghosh out of his mind?*" asked Khush as he pushed his iPhone towards Harry. "*Look at this quote,*" he said, referring to yet another controversial quote from the maverick.

Harry read it and smiled.

"*Why are you smiling? Isn't he mad?*" questioned Khush.

"*Sure, he is mad, he probably likes it that way.*" responded Harry.

"*Why do you say so?*" queried Khush.

"*I have read most of his quotes, they're all controversial. But he justifies his madness quite well.*" said Harry.

"*Really? How?*" asked Khush.

"*He says that good character and bad character is a subjective matter. Come to think of it,*" reasoned Harry, "*How do you judge one's character? He asks whether you prefer being judged by your morals or by ethics.*"

"*I see what you mean. One can understand good nature and bad nature. But behaviour, personality and characteristics are too abstract. You have no right to judge, simply because you are not in a position to.*" replied Khush.

"*So why give it so much importance?*" concluded Harry. "*On the other hand, health is well-defined and measurable. To maintain a good health, you need discipline, which comes from having a strong mind.*" he added.

"*That's Tapan Ghosh's view as well. He says that looking after your health is your prime goal.*" said Khush.

"*Absolutely! In fact, he has said several things about health, all of which are pertinent. Some of these may sound controversial, but the truth cannot be denied,*" commented Harry.

"*Do you remember his take on religion?*" asked Khush.

"Of course! He says that health is the only religion that matters. Every other religion is insignificant. Now, this may sound blasphemous, but this cannot be denied. You can't practice any religion if you are not in sound health." said Harry.

"He goes on to say that a true man of God is one who keeps himself physically, mentally, emotionally and spiritually healthy. Now, can anyone deny this?" continued Harry.

"Not at all. But tell me, how does one define health?" enquired Khush.

"Tapan Ghosh has an answer to this question too. Health is the sum total of physical well-being, mental stability, emotional soundness and finally, spiritual enlightenment. Can you beat that?" asked Harry.

"Wow! Tapan-da has studied health in acute detail. He has summed it up beautifully," remarked Khush. *"Does he say anything about its benefit?"*

"He says that sound emotional health can handle any crisis," said Harry.

"How true! But how does one keep fit?" enquired Khush.

"According to Tapan-da, to keep physically fit, listen to your own body, not to someone else. Unfortunately, we do the complete opposite. For example, the human body is designed in accordance with the laws of nature. The British left behind their potty which goes against these laws. It induces constipation, causes faecal stagnation, enlarges the prostate, leads to infection and weakens the muscles of the lower body," said Harry.

"Anything else that he suggests?" asked Khush.

"He has a lot of sound advice in this regard. As you open your eyes in the morning, the first thing to do is what a dog does. Stretch! Twists and turns are necessary to keep your body and mind fit. So is the case with your face; you are at liberty to make faces," recalled Harry.

"You mean, smile all the time, be cheerful," added Khush.

"Right! If you now link Tapan Ghosh's take on character - When character is lost, nothing is lost; when wealth is lost, something is lost; but when health is lost, everything is lost — to his thoughts on health, you will realise that he is talking sense. None of what he says is controversial or thoughtless. On the contrary, many who criticise him are out of their mind." concluded Harry with a smile.

CRAFTING ART IS INNOVATION

Storytelling

Narration with the camera is the art of connecting your audience to visuals and not words because body language conveys it all.

Expressing oneself is art, be it through singing, dancing, painting, writing or something else. But what comes most naturally are the spontaneous movements and gestures by which attitudes, and feelings are expressed with more clarity. Everyone inherently perceives this purity of body language that is acting. Each one of us is a born actor. How else can we survive in this wicked world?

Drama is a performing art, an outlet for self-expression. Performing arts - unlike visual arts such as painting - pertain to forms in which artists use their body language to communicate. It expresses the artist's emotions and feelings.

Unfortunately, most of this has now been commercialized in cinema. The big-screen projects a larger-than-life image and exudes glamour. With moviemakers seeking a global audience, budgets are magnanimous that makes producers and the middlemen - the so-called distributors – call the shots.

The performer is no longer himself; he has turned into a brand. The audience is hypnotized by a dramatic experience with which they are induced to hallucinate as if they were drugged. The addiction keeps the audience coming back for more. In this process of business-oriented filmmaking, the actual 'art' is completely ruined and lost.

Since time immemorial, art has educated the masses and satisfied the quest of the intellectuals. All of it is now enslaved to money. Authentic talent is dead. The need for rich and soulful beauty has been replaced by greed, the cause of all grief in the developed world today.

But Mother Nature never fails to strike a balance. The so-called swellheads who thought it to be their birth right to sit on their butts and slave-drive talent have been taken to task. The technology has turned the tables on them and digital era has taken the world by storm. Today, anyone who wants to tell a story merely needs a smartphone. The social media has given art the much-sought power to express itself.

It is a common knowledge now that traditional filmmaking has been subjected to heavy abuse by the established rogues of the film industry.

Millions of aspiring artists are exploited when all is decided by the bosses who have mastered the art of killing their talent.

So, what is the usual concept of making movies and how should it be modified?

A screenwriter writes a screenplay using someone else's life and experiences. The director tries to understand it, makes some changes and selects actors to fit the characters. The feasibility of this depends immensely on the basic nature; the characteristics; and the background. Fitting into a predefined character is a monumental task. The director tries to get the best out of the actors and the camera. Ultimately, it is the editor - with a personal perception - who decides on the final story.

Who is telling the story?

Too many cooks spoil the broth Resulting in a jumbled clutter.

Everyone shows himself to be the best. The unenviable task of handling ego clashes, conflicts, budget controls and schedules are assigned to the producer. He is the real captain who doesn't allow the ship to sink. Ultimately, the film's success depends on the calibre of the distributor who judges the film. Is this art?

No, it is arithmetic! Art, on the other hand, is about passion and expression.

How should this amendment be made?

There is no easy way to do this, but we all have the freedom to experiment with our smartphones, and I think most of us do exercise that.

I too did it my way, I'm essentially a storyteller, and right from my childhood, I have been questioned a lot. My responses were truthful, but hiding what others didn't want to hear, so there were a few twists. In the later phases of my life, I became a writer of prose and poetry. Very recently, I did what I wanted to do the most and that is to become an actor. And the only way out was to act in my movies, that too, to do it my way like everything else I've done in my life.

I do a visual script workshop which is an innovation with passion. There is no written script, only the premise and a structure, keeping that in mind, drawing on reality to make sure that every step moves towards the purpose of the premise.

All events are created on the spot, the participants, actions, and reactions studied, their performances examined. In short, it is about tracking the protagonist and the others with the camera. Editing is done by juxtaposing shots to make a scene, and scenes are joined together to make a movie. The story is straightforward.

We have made several such films. These have been uploaded on many digital platforms and have been well appreciated. Some of these are docudramas while others belong to the fiction genre.

There is a distinct advantage if the teller is an interpreter as well. So, I took the liberty to act in all my stories.

Actors cannot play a character unless they are able to adopt their traits, which is difficult and time-consuming. So, it is more effective to adopt the actor's individuality and construct a character around it. This gives the actor an advantage to be himself without attempting to be anyone else.

An actor is more natural when he speaks his mind than when he is trying to remember the lines. A narrator is at his best when his characters speak for themselves.

Furthermore, if he chooses to play a role, it is easier to influence others to play theirs as he sees fit. This innovative approach makes it an independent cinema that does not belong to the mainstream and thus more democratic and economically viable.

As a result, several companies have emerged to help filmmakers obtain independent films viewed and sold through the mainstream Internet.

With Internet film distribution, independent filmmakers who choose to forgo a traditional distribution agreement, now have the ability to reach a global audience.

To ensure nothing is left out, in simple statements I would like to summarize all that I have said and more.

Acting

- The real actor plays a double role in life.
- To live life to the fullest, you have to be a versatile actor to play all the roles.
- We are not puppets, but actors with the freedom to select our role, provided we adhere to His premise.
- How well an actor expresses himself is directly proportional to the freedom he gives to himself.
- An actor who is conscious of the camera ends up putting on an act.
- Actors who are conscious of their image cannot play anyone but themselves.
- Adapt to the situation like an actor and live life to the fullest.
- You have to be yourself to face the camera but an actor to face life.
- You have to be an actor to face life, the camera needs the real you.
- Acting is nothing more than the art of expression.
- Acting is all about expressing a character, not yourself.

Filmmaking

- The magic moments captured by the camera are the ones when your body language communicates the unconscious movements and postures along with the complementing attitudes, feelings, and tone.
- Moviemaking is the art of telling a story through actors who have

been molded into the characters.

- A moviemaker is essentially a storyteller.
- When a director makes a movie from a screenplay that is created from someone else's story, he is not the storyteller.
- Short films are distanced from glamour as today's youth identifies with reality.
- For short films to be realistic, we must mold the characters according to the actors and not the other way round.
- The job of a film producer is to bring objectivity to subjectivity.
- You are a film director only if you are an actor who follows God's directions and your destiny, which is His script.
- A film as a product is organic only if the director is a storyteller. The story should be his own; otherwise, it's just show business.
- You talk to the audience, not at them.
- Being the leader of the team, a director has to be good in all aspects of filmmaking. He is the origin, the storyteller.
- To mold a character around an actor is the job of a storyteller.
- The art of storytelling comes from your nightmares, not from your dreams.
- The beauty of a script lies in storytelling, which is sensed and felt without the barrier of language.
- Today's audience relates to spontaneity; shooting a story is better than writing it.
- If you can narrate a story in the first-person present tense, you have the skills of a scriptwriter.
- Imagination and writing skills are necessary to write a story but the matter comes from experience.
- A storyteller is an editor at heart and vice versa.
- A director must understand the person behind the actor to mold him into the character. To do so, he must be an actor first.
- A person who has faced life is easier to mold into a character than the one who has merely faced the camera.

Scriptwriting

- A writer should not introduce characters; they ought to reveal themselves.

- Character growth comes with faith and discipline.

- Character is the result of the relationship between your heart and mind.

- The easiest way to define character is to determine where one fits in, between the two extremes of sadism and masochism.

- Fiction is the reality couched to conceal the identity of the writer.

- Non-fiction is, in fact, fiction most of the time unless you live it before you write it.

- Impatience is a virtue if you have to write for today's generation.

- A novice writer reads a lot to learn to write. He would be better off thinking about what to write.

- A writer must live it up to capture the reader's imagination.

- The teachings of life should be the premise for writers.

- When you try to write, it is a deliberate act, and you lose out on the art.

- It is easier to jot down your thoughts when they emerge rather than forcefully try to write them.

- Even a writer has to balance the free mind and the controlled one, to put his thoughts into words. When in thought, the words don't come by, and when seeking words, the thoughts just vanish.

- Write what you feel, not what you see.

- Compartmentalizing your writing is not art.

- Writing a story is easy because the writer is doing all the talking in one language. There are no dialogues. Moreover, he writes what the characters think.

- Your life story is an episode of a beautiful script as long as you can watch yourself as a beholder.

- Each of us has a purpose in life. We need to know this and play our roles accordingly. Play your role well. Don't go against the premise of the story. Follow the best script writer in the world.

Who will give you as much flexibility as He does? He gives you the freedom to change your role and make the most of life.

- Why not make visual scripts instead of written ones?
- A fiction writer has to be multi-faceted unless it's a one-character story.
- A script should be like the plain truth that goes with the flow. It acquires a bias when penned.
- God does everything for us but with twists and turns. Life is a script!
- Scripts are better enacted than written.

Experimental cinema

A lot of us are experimenting to make videos on our smartphones and why not? There is a huge untapped talent available. We must liberate ourselves from our dependence on traditional cinema to make room for art and talent to prosper.

I have tried to do that in a small way.

Four short films have been published on YouTube so far and more to come. These zero-budget films have been scripted and shot in a day's time at available locations. It will be nice of you to support a good cause by putting your precious feedback.

Short films:

(Search these titles on YouTube or click the links for Kindle)

Ek Tarfa by Tapan Ghosh - https://youtu.be/IbItZH0NNdo

Shaadi Ka Licence by Tapan Ghosh - https://youtu.be/0eUcbDG-TpQ

Kuch Toh Log Kahenge by Tapan Ghosh - https://youtu.be/gULD1Hb6hWc

Pagalpanti by Tapan Ghosh - https://youtu.be/uCfWaLyQB4c